MW00488612

# DEMON'S DAUGHTER

## THE SENSITIVES BOOK FOUR

RICK WOOD

BLOOD SPLATTER PRESS

## ABOUT THE AUTHOR

Rick Wood is a British writer born in Cheltenham.

His love for writing came at an early age, as did his battle with mental health. After defeating his demons, he grew up and became a stand-up comedian, then a Drama and English teacher.

He now lives in Loughborough with his fiancé, where he divides his time between watching horror, reading horror, and writing horror.

# ALSO BY RICK WOOD

### The Sensitives:

*Book One – The Sensitives*

*Book Two – My Exorcism Killed Me*

*Book Three – Close to Death*

*Book Four – Demon's Daughter*

*Book Five – Questions for the Devil*

*Book Six - Repent*

*Book Seven - The Resurgence*

*Book Eight - Until the End*

### Shutter House

*Shutter House*

*Prequel Book One - This Book is Full of Bodies*

### Cia Rose:

*Book One – After the Devil Has Won*

*Book Two – After the End Has Begun*

*Book Three - After the Living Have Lost*

### Chronicles of the Infected

*Book One – Zombie Attack*

*Book Two – Zombie Defence*

*Book Three – Zombie World*

### Standalones:

*When Liberty Dies*

*I Do Not Belong*

*Death of the Honeymoon*

**Sean Mallon:**

*Book One – The Art of Murder*

*Book Two – Redemption of the Hopeless*

**The Edward King Series:**

*Book One – I Have the Sight*

*Book Two – Descendant of Hell*

*Book Three – An Exorcist Possessed*

*Book Four – Blood of Hope*

*Book Five – The World Ends Tonight*

**Non-Fiction**

How to Write an Awesome Novel

*Thrillers published as Ed Grace:*

**The Jay Sullivan Thriller Series**

Assassin Down

Kill Them Quickly

© Copyright Rick Wood 2018

Cover design by rickwoodswritersroom.com

Copy-edited by LeeAnn @ FirstEditing.com

With thanks to my Street Team.

No part of this book may be reproduced without express permission from the author.

*This book is dedicated to the memory of William Peter Blatty, without whom, exorcism horror would have just remained part of our nightmares.*

THEN

A THOUSAND SCREECHES SMOKED THROUGH A SINGLE THROAT. A throat smaller than your closed fist. A tender throat, not yet fully developed, roaring with fear and anger.

"Please!" Olivia cried, tears shredding her cheeks, then dancing into the surrounding gale. "Please, don't let it take her!"

Beside her quivering legs, the baby screamed its war cry. Multiple wails in multiple pitches, each one shattering the vertebrae, squeezing the ears, and wrenching the resolve of those hellbent few fighting this thing. Those stubborn, tightened minds stood around the innocent, youthful, unblemished face that did not represent what was beneath it.

They had to be ready to do what they dreaded.

After all, it only *looked* like a child.

Everything else about it was unnatural. Its eyes had an intensity behind them a child couldn't manage. Its fingers curled into a claw that could easily wrap around your throat. And, most peculiar of all, it was one month old, yet its body had developed as if it had lived for a year.

Martin was working harder than he felt able, exerting

energy his body was drained of. Father Jenson was by the young man's side, the grey strands surrounding his bald spot flickering in the hurricane that tormented the room. His body was ageing, but his resolve was equal to any other warrior that would defy this squealing wretch writhing beneath him.

The bedroom door shook. On the other side of it, the baby's father battled against its hinges, aggressive objections punching their way through the barricaded entrance.

In all honesty, Martin would be doing the same. The baby's daddy was full of rage, as any would be after their child was unknowingly ripped away and withheld from them. Martin fully expected that, should the father make it through the impossible mountain of furniture pushing back against that door, the lives of everyone in this room would be compromised in the man's endeavour to protect his child.

Martin, barely a few years into adulthood, found himself feeling foolish that he was the one guiding those in the room. He was closer to the baby's age than to that of those around him. Yet, he was the one with the innate ability, with the inherent, engrained power he couldn't deny. Just as Derek had told him: *you are the first and final defence in the fight against hell.*

Which meant he was the first and final defence against this counterfeit infant and the demon world its inhabitant had spawned from.

Father Jenson kissed his rosary and placed it around his neck. Patted down the vacant embroidery of his vestments. Took a deep breath in, and a long breath out.

"Father," Martin said, doing all he could to keep urgency from his voice; he could not allow Olivia to realise how close they were to losing. "We need to hurry."

Father Jenson nodded, kissed his fingers, and drew a cross in the air before his body.

"In the name of the Father, and of the Son, and of the Holy Ghost."

The baby's wretched mouth opened wider – so abnormally wide that, for a moment, Jensen expected it to swallow the room. Its persistent army of disordered vocal cords increased its salvo of screams even further. Its naked body wriggled against the blanket, its feeble hands with small fingernails flexing, its face scrunched into an upside-down mess.

This wasn't going to work.

Martin knew this wasn't going to work.

And he knew why.

He just couldn't tell them.

"Most glorious Prince of the heavenly armies..."

Martin couldn't interrupt Father Jenson's prayers to deliver such fateful news.

"...defend us in our battle against the power of the rulers of the darkness..."

Nor could Martin break Olivia's endless sobbing to inform her that there was no hope.

"...come to the assistance of men whom God has created in his likeness against the spirits of wickedness in all the high places..."

This was bad.

No, this was beyond bad. This was sick.

Only the deranged villains of hell would sink so low as to create such a devastating dilemma. To create such a horrible, detestable conundrum.

But those others in the room; they had no idea.

No idea there was no hope.

No idea that there was only one way out.

No idea that they were going to have to cease that infant's short, unlived life.

"...the holy church venerates you as her guardian and protector..."

Because it wasn't a child. It wore the skin of one, but what

3

squirmed and twisted and thrashed and blistered beneath was not made out of tissue, blood, and bone.

"...offer our prayers to the Most High, and without delay draw His mercy upon us..."

The baby wasn't possessed with a demon.

The baby *was* the demon.

"...His enemies are scattered..."

Olivia was the one who was possessed. And when she gave birth, she gave birth to that demon. The demon in human's clothing. Disguised with a face parents would protect with their own lives. Disguised with a face no one could bring themselves to think of as evil.

Disguised in a form it would be callous to destroy.

The dad battered against the door. He was under its spell. He knew nothing.

The priest. That was a lost cause.

Olivia. So full of hope that the son of heaven would have the solution.

Martin did have the solution. Only, it didn't involve the survival of her demented offspring.

"...as smoke is driven away–"

"Father, stop," Martin reluctantly demanded. His face dropped, paused, and lifted slowly toward the other two. "It's no good."

"What?" Father Jenson replied, fighting against the chaos of the room; the demon was using the elements to battle them and make the presence of its anger known, just as Martin had become accustomed to in has vast experience as an exorcist. "I've only just started!"

"It's no good. There's no demon inside the baby."

"No demon inside the baby! Look at the room, look at the child, can't you see it?"

Martin's eyes fixed onto Olivia's. Moist bags beneath her eyes. Bloodshot. Drained. Drooping optimism being willed to her eyes, glazing over in nothing but empty hope.

"Olivia, I –" Martin tried to say it, but he couldn't get past her name.

"What – what's happening to my baby?"

"Olivia, that is not your baby," Martin said, as matter-of-factly as he could. "That is a demon. There never was a baby; it's just been wearing the clothes of a child. An exorcism won't work. Nothing will work."

Olivia's hysteria overcame her. Her insatiable tears flew just as strongly as the manic contents of the room the demented entity spiralled into chaos.

"But how can that be?" Father Jensen asked. "I thought that if we–"

Before another word could be conversed, the unyielding hysteria from Olivia ceased, replaced by a determined growl. She grabbed the baby by the throat and launched herself forward. In the moment, Martin did nothing to stop her. He knew what needed to be done and hoped that he needn't be the one to do it. He felt guilty for taking pleasure in someone else assuming the responsibility of ending this demon's unnatural existence. But before this guilt could manifest, he had watched Olivia smash through the window, taking the wriggling, contorted mess with her.

Martin reached the windowsill, gripping his fingers into the ledge, peering below. Olivia lay on her back, groaning. Her leg appeared to be broken. But it hadn't worked.

The baby still wriggled beside her.

Olivia, struggling against the wild, conflicting emotions battling in her stomach, didn't even hesitate. A spare piece of shattered glass from the broken window lay beside her. She curled her palm around it. She ripped it back, into the air, and swung it downwards, sticking it into the tiny throat.

You may think her abrupt decision to do this was harsh.

You may even consider her act as a mother to be hideous. That for her to act in such a way without deeper consideration to be a heinous abuse of her responsibility as a mother. To take her child's life with such certainty is something you may label deranged, delusional, or even psychotic.

In which case, you do not know what you are talking about.

She had given birth to it. She had felt it inside her, the unnatural squirming of the dilapidated insect nibbling against her cervix. The horror of seeing its true form as it warranted the love of its father and the contempt of its mother. The way it willed everything and everyone around her to become evil.

No, she did what a good mother would do.

She killed it. Removed it from this world. Destroyed it before it could grow in strength, before it reached months old, before its hold over her husband had truly been taken. She took the godless creature from this earth before destruction could follow, before death and mayhem could ensue, before people would have to hurt, die, and worse, all as a result of her letting the child live.

What she did was the most loving act she could do. She removed what she had started. She prevented what it would potentially become.

And Martin, watching over the two bodies laid side by side, knew better than she did what could have happened if that demon in baby's clothing had been able to grow just a mere month older.

Its control on the world, its determination to take its mother's place on this earth, to carry out evil, genocidal deeds through manipulation of its father – all of it had been prevented.

If it had grown at all older, its power would have been too much.

They did what they had to do.

And they did it before it had been too late.

—————————

A DELICATE RIPPLE CARESSED THE LAKE. GENTLE SPLASHES OF water pushed along the surface, creating small lashes of droplets to sink into the bank. The clean stream floated along the narrow canal, reflecting the sun with a pleasant distortion.

Oscar saw April's hand hanging by her side. He wanted to take it, to sink his hand into hers, grasp it, clutch it. Everything in his body urged him to just try it, to reach out and see what would happen; but every time he built himself up to try, a wave of anxiety took over and he tapped out.

Most people like the early part of a relationship. Those early dates. When it's all new and exciting, with flutterings in the belly, an eagerness for memories to come. Most people relish the obsessive nature of their thoughts, the way that their focus centres solely around one person, their lips curving into a smile on the mere mentioning of a name, reminding them of that incessant longing to spend every waking moment either beside that one person – or between the sheets with them.

Oscar, however, did not like the early part of a relationship. Don't be mistaken, he adored April – every piece of her. He admired her hopeful gaze, her purple hair, her funky punkesque fashion. Her gumption. Her determination. The way she could still be caring and gentle, yet retain the demeanour of a strong, fiery woman. There wasn't a thing about her he wasn't falling in love with.

He was just so scared about losing that.

Those flutterings in his belly were not so much flutterings, but large, wriggling slugs exploding against his insides. Those thoughts of things to come were crashes of anxiety as he waited for her next text message to arrive, the same routine thrashing around his thoughts: *does she still like me? Why hasn't she texted back yet? Did I say something wrong in my text?*

And those moments between the sheets. He dreaded them. Not because he didn't enjoy them – if anything, they were the most blissful, amazing moments of his life. April's naked body was curved and smooth, with perfect contours entwined with perfect flesh. The activity between the sheets was electric, and he never wanted it to end.

He dreaded them due to his lack of experience in such things – his knowledge and application of sexual activity so far had been mostly in the privacy of his own company, whereas he suspected April's experience was somewhat more rounded. Though he never had the guts to ask her. Maybe he was being presumptuous; but if he wasn't, he didn't really want to know.

So he tried to calm his racing thoughts. His desperate insecurities. His manic ego. And he just focussed on one thing.

Her vacant hand.

"You know," she said, "you can hold it if you like."

Oscar couldn't help but chuckle. Could she really read him so easily?

Or had he just been staring at that hand for the last five minutes?

Either way, it didn't matter. He slid his hand gently into hers and his entire body grew warm, like a hot water bottle had grown to his height and encapsulated him in its tranquillity.

"I love this lake," April told Oscar. "I used to come here as a kid. Before, you know, there were any issues. My dad would bring a picnic. And then he'd let us go swim in it. Though we'd have to do so naked."

"You were naked?" he retorted.

"Relax, Oscar, I was two."

Both April's beautiful and tragic memories highlighted to Oscar how much had happened in the twenty-one years before he entered her life. He scolded himself for his unrestrained pang of jealousy, and quickly quelled it. He just had to accept that April had a life before him.

*But what if that life turns out to have been better?*

"I came here again, when I was on the streets. Slept under a bridge further up. It wasn't as nice, but it gave me some kind of comfort. I guess you could say it's my special place."

"Well," replied Oscar, willing the bad thoughts away. "I'm pleased that you have brought me to your special place."

She turned toward him, placing her arms tightly around his chest. He was taller than her, meaning that she had to squint due to the sun beaming behind his head.

"Now it's *our* special place," she told him.

Her face lifted, and her lips sank into his like velvet against silk. His heart quickened pace, his whole body tingled, and his mind was temporarily at ease.

"You know how much I care about you, right?" April said, leaving her forehead resting on his.

"What do you mean?"

"I know we've not been dating long, but I just…"

"Just what?"

She held his eye contact. Peered at him with her big, blue eyes, her hair flickering in the gentle summer's breeze.

"I'm in love with you," she told him.

And that was it.

The moment.

Where life as Oscar knew it halted. The gentle waves in the lake crashed around him, placing him in an eternal trance. Holding him rigidly where he was, his feet part of the floor, his knees shaking.

And, in that moment, every insecurity disappeared. Every worry about her not texting him back, every worry about what guys may have come before, every worry about anything that stopped him from enjoying every moment he had with her.

She was in love with him.

She was happy.

And she'd told him she'd never been in love before. Which meant he was the first.

And the last.

And everything in between.

"I am so in love with you, too," Oscar returned.

Their lips matched in perfect synchronicity once more.

Of course, Oscar felt stress in their relationship at random moments of insecurity. Who doesn't? But that constant anxiety, that frequent voice at the back of his mind that bullied him, that manifested his insecurities into big monsters that stopped him from relishing the good memories they were creating – that left.

It was replaced with a sense of purpose. Of unconditional love. Of a euphoria that could be caused simply by the thought of her, replacing any worry that would have previously been there.

This was the point at which Oscar wished his life could just freeze in time.

But it's never as simple as that.

Is it?

NOW

## 3

Beep. Beep. Beep.

Normally an incessant noise such as this would be the cause of irritation. You would seek it out with intention to eradicate it, to destroy it, to make it cease; allowing you to continue with your activities unperturbed.

But for Oscar, this sound was his salvation.

It was the sound that meant April was still alive.

Her eyes remained shut, but her chest still rose and fell in perfect rhythm. Her hand didn't return Oscar's squeeze, but her fingers still twitched. And whilst her mouth didn't open, her lips still gently pursed with such a subtle movement, Oscar was sure he was the only one who saw it. Her body tucked into bedsheets absent of colour, her hair spread across the pillow, her feet dressed in her favourite slipper socks.

The sterile hospital walls had been her home for months. More recently, there had been suggestions of more long-term plans. What would happen should her eyes never open.

Oscar wouldn't entertain a word of it.

He knew she was still in there. She wasn't lost. She was a fighter, and he had no doubt she would be fighting for every inch of life. She was more than just a girl in a bed – she was the strongest woman he knew. He had always needed her more than she needed him. She had always been the one who gave him the strength to continue. Who had faith in him, even when he had little himself.

Now it was time for him to return the sentiment.

He brushed hair from her eyes. The tips of her strands remained purple, but her roots were beginning to show the true brunette that hid beneath. He squeezed a ball of dry shampoo in his hands and fed it through her hair.

Her eyelids flickered, and he held his breath. This could be it. She could wake up.

But, just like last time, and the time before that, and the time before that – she did not.

But it was promising. Flickering eyelids were a sign that someone is dreaming. He didn't know where he'd heard such information, and, honestly, he didn't care – he latched onto it, not letting go of the solitary thought that gave him hope.

He brushed her teeth. Brushed her hair. Changed her clothes.

Did everything he could to keep her fresh and healthy.

Then he turned behind him. He looked at the reason April was comatose. The heavenly, wonderful, gracious reason staring back at him.

The child.

Oscar and April's daughter, Hayley, who had survived an incredibly complicated birth, a birth that had taken April's conscious state from her.

This child was the reason April was as she was, but that didn't change how much Oscar loved and adored her.

Hayley hobbled over toward Oscar, smiling up at him.

She was a genius. A miracle.

He couldn't explain her life so far. It was curious, incredible, and completely extraordinary.

What he had witnessed, he could not put into words. By the end of Hayley's first month of life, a month where he still expected to be cradling her in his arms, feeding her from a bottle, responding to her desperate tears – she had already grown so far beyond that. She had crawled, then she had walked. By the end of her first month she looked and acted like a one-year-old.

And that's the speed with which she continued to grow.

He hadn't accepted it at first. How could he? It was bizarre. But then he considered: *she is the daughter of two Sensitives, is she not?*

Heaven had supposedly conceived both him and April. To create a child with the powers and ability they both had, how could they not expect to form something miraculously special?

And now, here she was. A four-month-old child with the body of a four-year-old. Balancing herself on her two sturdy legs. Smiling and interacting with Oscar in a way he never could have predicted. In fact, her lack of ability to talk was the only indication that she wasn't as old as she seemed. When Oscar was at the park and other parents asked how old she was, he stopped bothering to tell them the truth. Numerous times, he'd felt like carrying around her birth certificate just to prove it.

He wondered, for a moment, what would happen in the next few years. At eighteen months, would she already be an adult? What would happen with school – how would she learn what she needed to in that short time? Would this mean that her life would end up being shorter – or would her life end up in some way they could not foresee? Could she become something special – something magical?

Yes, he knew the rapidity of her growth had been strange, her development bizarre, her cognitive abilities unprecedented. It was irregular, yes, but Oscar didn't take any notice of scepticism; he simply enjoyed being the father of the fast-growing genius that baffled doctors. And, boy, did doctors want to meet her! They fought each other for the opportunity to see her, anything to study this evolutionary triumph; to find out why and how, to speculate as to what gave her this ability to advance at a higher rate than any other child they had seen. She was a marvel.

To Oscar, she was just Hayley.

His little girl who was growing up so fast. She was proving to be remarkable, and Oscar had made the decision that it wasn't up to him to ask why. It was up to him just to love her and accept whatever quirks and eccentricities she may have.

Hayley placed her soft, delicate hands against the bed beside her mother's comatose body. She gazed upon April's face.

An unusual expression adorned her. Oscar couldn't decipher it. It was a look of love, but there was something more… devious…about it. Something primitive that made her look even older. As if she was happy to see her mother, but for some kind of sinister reason.

Oscar knew he was overthinking.

His child was perfect.

Perfect.

Completely, and utterly–

"Mama," she said.

Oscar's hands fired to his mouth.

"What did you just say?" he gasped.

Hayley smiled at her daddy.

"Mama," she repeated.

"Oh my God!"

Her first word.

At four months.

He'd read books… books about parenting… about what to expect…

Twelve to sixteen months, they had said…

Sixteen months…

And now, there she was. Not just speaking, but able to identify who the person was laid before her.

How had she managed that?

She was…a genius.

The only explanation.

A remarkable, pure, loveable genius.

"You are so smart!" Oscar told her, crouching and wrapping his arms around her. "So smart! So, so smart!"

Hayley smiled back at him. Her infantile, chubby cheeks bursting indefinable affection to her primary caregiver.

"You are right, that is your mama. That's Mummy. Do you recognise her? Do you?"

Hayley nodded.

Walking. Talking. Interacting.

*At four months!*

She was a genius.

A genius.

*An unnatural genius.*

And she was an *unnatural genius* – but only one of those words registered with Oscar.

The word *genius* made him grin. It was all he could see.

The word *unnatural* – that was the word he should have been lamenting. The word he should have been considering and contemplating, as deeply as he could, analysing and picking apart and dissecting it until he realised that the whole rapid development was exactly that – *unnatural*.

But a father's love is its own blindfold.

And to Oscar, she was a genius.

And to April, she was something else.

He planted a gentle kiss on the love of his life, took his daughter's hand, and walked out of the room. As they left down the corridor, Hayley did not lose her footing once.

## 4

SUPERMARKET SHOPPING HAD NEVER REALLY BEEN SOMETHING Oscar looked forward to. There was that initial excitement when he first moved out of his parents' house, that immediate thought of – "Wow, I shop for myself and buy whatever food I want!" – but, as most 'adult' routines do, it turned from an exciting experience of independence to an annoying routine fairly quickly. In truth, April used to be the one who did the shop. Oscar would be coerced into going, but his role would usually be to follow around and positively affirm April's suggestions.

There was one thing that made the activity enjoyable – Hayley.

He watched with hidden glee at other parents having to navigate a shopping trolley in one hand and the wrist of a hyperactive, unhelpful child in the other. The masses of screaming children, of single parents begging for a moment of peace, making promises of a treat if they – would – just – shut – up – for – a – moment.

Hayley was an angelic splice of delight. She held onto the side of the trolley and followed Oscar's lead without a word of dismay or protest. When Oscar paused, he could feel her wayward eyes drifting toward him, looking up at him with that proud look he would often return. Every moment they took in the supermarket was another moment of smugness that passing droopy-eyed parents envied as they absentmindedly wandered around in their zombie-like state, ignoring their child's constant demands.

Even as Oscar reached the checkouts, he had barely moved before Hayley had begun unloading the trolley for him. Not just in the random, attempting-to-be-helpful way that a child may resort to when trying to be useful, much like the way he would unload a trolley after following April around for half an hour. No, Hayley loaded the food with perfect organisation. Heavy vegetables were at the front, tins next, then boxes, subdivided into frozen and not frozen, then softer packages. It was as if she'd watched Oscar do it, picked up the way it was done, and repeated it perfectly.

*Wow,* Oscar thought. *That girl is so perceptive.*

Oscar joined in the unloading of the trolley. It took him a while to notice that Hayley had stopped unloading.

"What's the matter?" he asked.

Hayley didn't move.

"Hayley?" he prompted.

Still, nothing.

Her eyes were open wide, staring at a fixed spot to Oscar's right. The rigidity with which they were fixed unsettled Oscar. It was like she was in a trance.

His gaze altered course, looking across the subsequent checkouts, trying to see what she was focussed on. Across the aisles, various shoppers unloaded their shopping, just as Oscar had been. Person after person, in their own world, no awareness of anyone else.

So, what was she so fixed on?

He put a hand on her shoulder and gave her a slight shake.

She didn't move. Her eyes didn't blink.

An exaggerated moan caught Oscar's attention. It sounded like someone had stood on a piece of glass, a moan of pain and surprise twisted with unexpected anger.

A few heads turned, then resumed their shopping.

Then the noise came again.

And again.

People started to snap out of their absentminded unloading, ceasing their mechanical actions, turning in the direction of the guttural groans.

Approaching from the shadows of the far door was a man. At least, Oscar thought it was a man. The person's head was too disguised with greased strips of hair, strips that both covered the guy's face and stuck statically in every wayward position possible. His walk was less of a walk, and more of a hobble; a slant to one side, like someone doing a poor job of imitating a zombie. Their movement lagged, moving closer at a steady speed, but moving closer nonetheless. And their eyes, accentuated by dark-grey bags and extravagantly feral eyebrows, were fixed on those of Oscar's daughter.

"Hayley, stop," he prompted.

The man screamed again. He was a few checkouts away, steadily gaining ground, his grunts tearing through the shocked shoppers with an animalistic intensity.

"Hayley, come on."

Her eyes remained transfixed.

The grunt repeated itself, but in that grunt, there were words – Oscar just couldn't make them out.

"Ayeeyoo!" the oncoming man barked. His clothes were a charcoal-grey and black, stiffened with dirt, hairy feet exposed beneath the frayed ends of his trousers.

Hayley took a step back.

"Ayts oo!"

Oscar stood in front of Hayley.

"Ayts you!"

"What?"

"Ayt's you!" the man's words loosely formed.

"Back off," Oscar instructed.

A security guard finally intervened, placing a hand on the man's arm. The man was not deterred. He continued to shuffle toward Hayley.

"Itez yhoo!"

"Come on now," instructed the beefy security guard. "Time to go."

"No-yyy-eee-ow!" the man retorted, his distant expression curling into a mark of aggression.

The security guard began pushing the man toward the exit. The man tried to fight but there wasn't enough of him to contest his presence; he looked starved, his skin clinging tightly to his bones. The security guard didn't need to use any strength, settling for gently coercing the man into changing his direction, though the man uselessly tried to resist, his hands flailing out, reaching out, desperately clambering, noises continuing to fire out his mouth.

"Nyoo! Groff mooe! Itez yhoo!"

Oscar watched the man being taken outside. The guy didn't let up. He bashed against the window with a weak persistence, tried to get back in, but the security guard stood firm and still. Throughout the whole ordeal, his eyes did not move from their focus, still surveying the same person.

"Sir?" came the woman at the checkout, abruptly snapping Oscar out of his gaze.

"Oh, sorry," Oscar said, presenting his card to pay.

He looked to Hayley, who was happily packing his bags.

He looked to the door. No one there.

The security guard was back at his station, monitoring CCTV.

All the shoppers around him had continued with their routine lives.

It was as if nothing had happened.

As if someone had entered his brain and changed the scene. Like someone had reached in and placed people, as if they were toys, in a position that looked natural, then said nothing.

Hayley was smiling again. Happy, oblivious child. Unaware.

Oscar shrugged it off and continued with his day.

## 5

THE STEAM OF TWO CUPS OF COFFEE ROLLED UPWARDS AND turned to nothing. Oscar and Julian took a simultaneous sip as they encouraged their minds to wander, for their thoughts to find solutions.

Julian watched Oscar with dubious curiosity. Oscar looked over his shoulder, through the doorway to the living room, where Hayley sat peacefully at a small child's table. Her crayons scribbled with enthusiasm over the paper below her.

Julian noticed how the crayon she was using was red.

Oscar caught Julian's eye looking at his daughter and smiled proudly.

"Great, isn't she?" Oscar said.

"Oh, yeah," Julian replied dryly, trying not to let his true feelings be known. "She's great."

"The things she can do, they are just amazing."

Julian studied Oscar as he took another sip of his coffee.

"Like what?"

"Like, she's already walking. And without any help. She's parading all over the place. She's like her mother."

"How's that?"

"How's what?"

"How's she like her mother?"

Oscar beamed as he considered the question. "Curious. Intelligent. Ahead of her time, in a way."

"Tell me," Julian began, not knowing how to say what he had to say, but knowing he somehow needed to say it. "What age is a child supposed to start walking?"

"The books said, like, a year onwards."

"And she's, what, how old?"

"Four months."

"And she's already walking?"

"Yep."

"What, like wandering around, balancing perfectly, without any help from you?"

"Completely."

"Doesn't that seem a bit…unnatural?"

Oscar's positive demeanour momentarily fell. A wave of perplexity crossed his face, and he turned back to Julian with a smile of resistance.

"I know what you're trying to do," Oscar observed.

"What's that?"

"Everything I do, you put a damper on it. I could save the world and you would say I got lucky. And now I have a daughter – an *amazing* daughter – who is practically a genius. And you're not taking that away from me."

Julian leant forward.

"I'm just saying, Oscar, it isn't genius, it's strange. Impossible, even. It's–"

"Look," Oscar interjected, raising a hand into the air. "I miss April. I miss her *so* much. And you're her oldest friend, I get it. But don't take that out on my daughter. My daughter doesn't deserve it."

Julian considered this for a moment. Yes, he missed April. There hadn't been a day for over ten years when he hadn't seen her. But Oscar's assessment of things was uncharacteristically off. Whatever disagreements had occurred between them, Oscar was still fairly consistent at being able to assess a situation. Yet with Hayley, logic didn't seem to appeal to him.

*She is four months old.*

And Julian knew four months was too early to be able to walk, or interact on the level she could, or be as physically developed as she was. Way too early. But Oscar didn't even seem open to the suggestion.

But then again, what was Julian suggesting?

April's pregnancy had been beyond complicated – toward the end, there had been a certainty that it was unnatural. Julian could vividly remember the fear about what was going to come out of April once she gave birth. All that terror, that dread that some hideous beast was going to rip her apart from the inside, that she was going to be mother to something from hell. Then this...baby...came out. A normal, healthy baby. That placed its healthy mother in a coma that doctors can't explain.

Oscar seemed to have forgotten about everything that had led up to Hayley's birth.

Julian could understand it. Every father is proud. But there's pride, then there's delusion.

And this gifted child just seemed to be too gifted.

She seemed to be...

"So, we going to sort this out then, or what?" Oscar said, interrupting Julian's thoughts.

"Oh, yeah, sure," Julian responded, opening a folder onto the desk.

"So, what's the problem?"

"We're losing money. The business is lacking clients. Without April's expertise, we lose a huge part of the service we can offer."

Oscar took the folder and looked over the various spreadsheets Julian had prepared.

"So, how long are we safe for?"

"We've got enough money for a few months. But, if things don't change, then we're going to have to–"

"Things *will* change."

Oscar held Julian's eye contact.

Oscar was always the optimist. Julian hated it then more than ever – it always seemed to be Julian's role to 'say it as it is.' To be the one who's direct, blunt, the truth-teller. The one who puts aside useless hopefulness to bring a matter of reality to the situation. And, yes, April could wake up at any moment; yes, there's nothing wrong with her – but what if she doesn't?

What then?

Oscar continued to make his way through the paperwork, surveying the figures and numbers. Looking through the past client list. Through the booked clients. Through the finances. Everything that gave him a better idea where they were.

As Oscar did this, Julian found his gaze rising to another pair of eyes from the living room.

Funny, isn't it – how we can always tell when someone is staring at us. Like our subconscious is somehow aware.

But this was something more.

As Oscar worked, oblivious to it, Julian and Hayley's stare locked into place.

Julian felt sick.

Something in his belly twisted. Made him nauseous. Made him want to throw up.

Then his head. Pulsating. As if his brain was convulsing. Throbbing against his skull entrapment. Seizing.

A sudden migraine pounded through his mind.

Hayley smiled.

And turned back to her drawing.

Julian knew what this was. He knew all too well.

It was a warning.

A war cry.

A demonstration of the consequences of Julian's defiance.

"I don't know what to say," Oscar said. "This looks bad."

"Don't worry about it, let me figure it out. You said you had to take Hayley somewhere?"

"Yeah, she's going to see her grandparents."

"Well, leave it to me for now."

Julian watched as Oscar stood, took Hayley's hand, and guided her to the bottom step, where he helped her put on her shoes.

Not that she needed it. But she allowed it. Allowed Oscar to think that he was being useful in his fatherly duty.

Allowed him to think that she needed him.

After they had gone, Julian made his way to the living room to tidy up the colouring. As he did, he picked up sheet, after sheet, after sheet, after sheet of coloured-in pieces of paper.

Each one of them completely covered in red.

## 6

THE JOURNALS OF DEREK LANSDALE. DAYS OF READING lay scattered across the table, like it had been many times before, and would be many times again. Some of it riveting. Some of it Derek's lengthy waffle.

But always – or, most of the time, at least – a source of answers.

*And without Derek here anymore...*

Julian hesitated. Let the thought wash over him and pass. Grief never suited him. Sure, there was an absence he wouldn't acknowledge; a discomfort he ignored. But he wouldn't let it win. He only allowed himself to dwell on sorrowful thoughts in brief, momentary lapses of self-control, then he let them drop off him, like letting go of a heavy bag, or removing clothes drenched in rainwater.

It hurt.

It stung.

Then he closed his eyes.

And it was gone.

Julian placed the next journal in front of him and found the index. Derek had been a great many things to many different people; wise, thoughtful, occasionally deluded. But one thing Derek was, without a doubt, was organised – meaning that his many, many journals had been thoroughly indexed, with not a detail missed. Recurring themes and demons were identified, and their locations clearly dictated in a comprehensive alphabetised list. The year, the pages, occasionally even the lines. Some might say that putting such a thing together was a task you would undertake only if you were very, very bored – but Julian would say that those people did not know Derek Lansdale.

He twirled the end of his pen between his teeth.

What exactly was he searching for in these journals?

Something that could relate to Hayley?

But what? What precisely would Derek have experienced that could come close to the suspicions Julian held? What could one even look up to find such a reference?

He'd already read the pages on demon births, including the pages that Derek had originally omitted out of shame. What else could he look for next?

He considered this for a moment. Ignoring the wave of nostalgia Derek's scribbly-yet-legible handwriting forced upon him. Ignoring anything at all that may require an emotional reaction.

Demon baby, maybe?

He navigated the dusty pages to D, then to demon – where he found multiple references to the word, followed by multiple subcategories.

He followed them down.

*Demon Aztec.*

*Demon Azkar.*

*Demon Baal*

*Demon Babilon*

Beneath the entry where he expected to see the reference were the following words:

*Demon Banshee.*

Julian stared in bemusement. He re-read the lines a few times. Checked the nearby lists, whether the alphabet had been haphazardly applied, whether the word had been miswritten elsewhere.

Of course, it hadn't. This was Derek's indexing. It was bulletproof.

Julian was initially astonished, then sceptical. How could Derek have gone through decades of work in the paranormal and not come across a baby with demonic inclinations? It seemed so unlikely.

Then again, Derek had omitted pages before.

But that was just the once. Surely.

"Hmm," Julian pondered.

He looked for another keyword.

*Demon chains.*

*Demon chef.*

*Demon chivalry.*

*Demon change.*

Just where he expected to find it, again, there was no *Demon child.*

He slammed the index shut.

His patience was up.

His patience being up seemed to be a far more frequent occurrence in the past few months, but what the hell; he was the only one bothering. Oscar was off with his happy child. April was off with the clouds.

And where was Julian?

*Researching whether my best friend's child is a sodding demon.*

He stood, knocking the chair over as he did. Threw the pen across the room. Punched the wall, hurt his knuckles, winced in pain.

Why was he so angry?

He was fully aware that, as a person, he could be, at times, ill-tempered – but this permanent state of anger he felt within himself in was too much. Everything infuriated him. Full of rage. Full of fire.

And he had no one to tell it to.

No one except the faded pages of a deceased man's journal.

But pages don't listen. All they do is tell.

THEN

## 7

Martin's arms remained folded and his expression deadened. He refused to show emotion. Emotions meant weakness. He was beyond that.

At the front of the church stood a priest, talking about how great Madeleina was. Embellishing about her kindred spirit. Her enthusiastic nature. Her infectious personality.

How the hell would he know?

He never met her.

Never held hands with her. Never went weak by her smile. Never watched her when she cried, rubbed her shoulders when she was aching, or watched her cry with happiness when she found out she was pregnant.

Pregnant.

She was–

The exorcism of the infant a few days ago still played in his mind like a broken film reel going round and round and round. Coughing up grainy pictures. But as grainy as they got, the clarity of the situation did not falter.

Was there anything else he could have done?

The baby wasn't a baby. It was a demon. It had to die. It had to. It was...

The priest drew the curtain around the coffin. Everyone stood. Some looked down, some looked up, some looked into their open palms as their bodies shuddered, disguising their tears.

Martin didn't look anywhere but at the curtains, keeping a stern face, watching intently as the drapes billowed out, rising a few feet off the ground and hovering there.

He didn't turn away.

As the fire turned Madeleina's body to ashes, his unborn child with it, he kept his eyes rigidly fixed to that damn curtain.

Cremation always felt so final. Like there was no way back. Like, wherever they were, that's where they were staying. They had no body they could use anymore.

That question repeated itself.

Was there anything else he could have done?

Madeleina had been pregnant. With his child. But something had plagued the pregnancy, something evil, something sinister had taken hold of her and driven her to suicide. She was a happy person, always laughing, joking, never depressed – and this demon had ripped that out of her, had shoved its vile claw down her dry throat and ripped out her goodness.

Derek had believed it was the baby that was the source of her dismay. That the baby was somehow evil. Somehow demonic.

What if this baby had been the same as Olivia's?

What if this baby had turned out to be nothing of the sort?

What if Derek had done the right thing by encouraging them to be rid of it?

What if...

Those stupid two words again.

*What if. What if. What if.*

They are said so much, yet accomplish nothing. Hypothesising is just that – a useless, endless, onslaught of questions that no one answers.

Tears became background noise. The curtain billowed out further. As if this was it, the point that her soul left.

And the soul of his dead baby.

If it had a soul.

In his eyeline, he caught sight of a familiar face.

Derek. The man he'd said he never wanted to see again. The man who had ruined this for them. The man who had been there when Madeleina had…

He may have been doing the right thing.

Martin wrenched his face into a twisted contortion, willing the thought away, punching the notion that Derek was right out of his mind.

He may have been.

But to hell with him anyway.

The curtain dropped.

The fire ended.

The room was still.

But Derek remained. His head solemnly bowed. Paying his respect.

His respect to the woman that he watched jump to her death. The woman that Martin had loved. The woman that had–

*Stop.*

With a snarl of contempt, Martin turned and left the church. He walked fast, direct, carrying himself forward with desperate haste. An aimless march between the graves and out of the gravel path, onto the street. Between houses, allotments, and playschools. Between homes, gardens, and nurseries. Between all those pieces of happiness that wrecked his vision. Those places he couldn't have. Would never have.

Tears fell.

What if the baby had been like Olivia's?

What if his baby hadn't even been a baby at all?

The child was doing something to its mother. Was twisting her insides, turning her soul inside out, pushing through her mind. Destroying the woman she was.

When she died, she was a wreck.

How could he have seen it coming?

How could he have done anything different?

His phone beeped. He checked it.

It was the update he had expected, but still dreaded.

Olivia was being charged with murder. With murder of her own child. Her own baby.

What a justice system we have. Condemning a mother for destroying a demon because it refuses to acknowledge what so many of us keep tied up in a secret inside. A whole society based on denial.

How dare Derek show up.

How dare he show his face at Madeleina's funeral.

How dare he.

How dare he.

How dare.

How...

He fell to his knees. His suit trousers ripped and gravel cut his knee, but he didn't care. His head buried in his hands. Passers-by crossed the road to avoid him. An idiot in a car honked a horn and shouted something. It was all just noise.

It was far away.

Somewhere else.

Martin was encapsulated in his arms.

He had to stop this. Be strong. Carry on.

For Olivia.

For Madeleina.

For himself.

But first, he allowed himself to feel.

And he felt every single part of it.

NOW

## 8

She watched Oscar.

Watched him carefully.

Lovely Oscar.

Impeccable man.

Foolish Daddy.

She followed him down the path. Staring at the back of his knees as they waddled forward.

Pretending.

Walking slower. Can't walk too fast.

Stupid Daddy.

Slow down. Not supposed to be able to walk this fast.

Stumble a bit.

That's it.

Idiot Daddy.

Around the corner they turned. A man with a moustache greeted Oscar. Shook his hand. Spoke to him. Spoke about what breed he was looking for. What he was after.

"Just, I don't know, something good around kids," he said.

Something good around kids.

The thought revolved around her head.

*He's talking about me.*

The man with the moustache smiled at her. That patronising smile adults save only for children. Wider than normal smiles. Bigger eyebrow expression. Big, childish smile.

She'd rip that smile off dig claws in dig deep press through thread the needle rip hard rip harder pull his teeth out make him eat them shove them down his throat until he coughs on blood coughs more coughs until he chokes until he vomits until he lays limply spasming as the final moments of life are ripped out of him *and I would watch his soul as it left his body wrap my claws around it and drag it down to hell I wish in time but I can't because I'm being a good girl a good girl I'm being a good sweet pathetic little girl.*

She smiled sweetly back at him.

"Adorable child," the moustache man told Oscar.

"I know," Oscar replied. Gave her a wink only they share. Beaming with pride. With love.

She had him.

She knew she had him.

Senseless Daddy.

"This way," moustache man said, Oscar following, and she followed, pretending to find the pavement difficult because it's uneven, finding it a nuisance, what a nuisance, a terrible nuisance.

Stumble. Whoops. Slower.

They entered a pen with cages – she loved cages – dogs behind each one. They slept, they stood, they wagged their tales, they jumped up to see the visitor. Eager, enthusiastic companions of man.

Oscar marvelled at them. Bent down to say hello as if they were innate idiots.

Then they looked at her.

They all looked at her.

And Oscar saw that they looked at her.

And then the howling. The ear-shredding howling, filling the room with such a deafening volume Oscar had to put his hands over his ears, then over her ears – mustn't damage her young ears – unable to hear the moustache man talk about how he doesn't understand because they are never like this and why are they like this, this is so strange.

She made eye contact with each of them.

Each and every one.

And she knew.

And she threatened.

"Shut up!" she screamed. "Shut up or I will rip your fucking insides out!"

But it didn't come out.

Because she couldn't let it.

She couldn't talk. Not yet. Soon. But not yet.

So she looked back.

And they knew.

They knew that she would rip their furry paws off the bone and wedge them down their yuppity throats until that high-pitched whine like a toy that talks but has a dying battery passes out of them until they stop being man's faithful friend and be his limp crushing cross to bear until they burn and burn *and fucking burn everyone will burn everyone ever in the world and I will eat their fucking meatbag child until their fucking limp hands drop from their parents' clammy claws and fade into submission and I have them all in my jaw and they all fucking burn all fucking burn and* she wished that these dogs would just shut up their shouting.

So they did.

All at once, their crescendo ceased. The chorus stopped singing, their voices halted, their manuscript reached the end.

She looked at Oscar.

Wiped it. Wiped his acknowledgement that they all stared at her as they shouted. That there was anything peculiar about this situation at all. That there was any reason why he should worry.

Why he should worry about himself.

Or April.

His precious April.

*April.*

"You know," Oscar said with a sense of resolution, "I'm not sure about this."

"Really?" moustache man replied.

"No, I mean, I was hoping to get one for my girlfriend when she…but never mind. Maybe it's not the best idea."

And he took hold of her hand and led her out and she let him and it felt like sick but she showed him it was love because that's what he needed to believe.

And she sat in the car seat.

And she smiled all the way home.

Like a good little girl.

A good little girl.

Good. Little. Girl.

## 9

OSCAR HELD APRIL'S HAND THE WAY HE ALWAYS HELD APRIL'S hand. Tightly, between both of his. A grip of affection capturing her soft skin in his warmth.

Then he brushed her hair like he always did, washed her face like he always did, and sat and moped like he always did.

Hayley stood in the doorway, her back to him. Staring. Like she often did. Staring across the corridor toward the children's ward. No doubt engrossed in the actions of other children, in seeing children like her, but different; more pale, more bony, less lively.

He let her stay there. She wasn't hurting anybody. And intrigue in a child was a good thing.

It meant he could have his moment alone, undisturbed.

He willed himself to contain his tears. To keep them locked in the corner of his eyes. Enough of tears. They occur too often, and for what? They don't change anything. Just make his cheeks red and his face pathetic.

No, the tears can stay inside.

It just hurt so, so much.

She shifted, and Oscar leapt to his feet, full of spritely

energy – but it was nothing. Barely even a shudder. A larger breath that flickered a loose strand of hair from her face. Her huff left the strand wayward. On the pillow, disjointed from her locks that Oscar had neatly groomed.

"Good morning," came a voice Oscar was becoming uncomfortably used to.

"Hi," Oscar said, his voice low, his tone limited. His eyes remained on the love of his life.

Doctor Starley entered the room, a chart in his hand. He entered slowly, as if this was a sacred space he was disturbing and he wished to be cautious.

"How are we today?" Starley asked.

Oscar glanced at Hayley, still distracted by the children's ward across the corridor.

Oscar went to say fine, then chose not to. What was the use in being obtuse?

"I've been better," he said, favouring honesty over positive face.

Starley stepped forward and placed the chart in its slot at the end of April's bed. He went to say something, but his open mouth lapsed and his lips shut again.

"You've got nothing new to tell me, have you?" Oscar asked, guessing why Starley was not so forthcoming in conversation.

"I'm afraid not," Starley replied after a breath of reluctance.

"Is there even a guess? A hypothesis? Some idea what's even going on?"

Starley sighed. Considered his thoughts. Perused his potential words with care.

Oscar scoffed. That was the answer he needed.

"We are doing all we can," Starley offered.

"Yeah, well," Oscar groaned, then decided not to finish his honest feedback.

"There's just no explanation, I'm afraid. She is perfectly

healthy. Her heart is beating, her brain is active, our scans don't show the activity of someone asleep or comatose."

Oscar kept his eyes on April's lips, poised in purgatory between a smile and a frown.

"It's an anomaly," Starley said. "Pure and simple. And I know it's not what you want to hear, but it is. And we are doing all we can to solve it, but every so often, every one in a million, we get them – anomalies."

"And what exactly do you define as an anomaly, Doctor?"

"Ah, well…a patient that shows no obvious symptoms. No causes. No similarities between that patient and others in the same situation. The patient is a case completely isolated, on their own. And that is how you should treat that patient."

Oscar winced at the third mention of the word *patient*.

This wasn't a patient.

To the doctor, maybe, yes.

But to Oscar she was the best thing that ever happened to him. Mother of another amazing feature of his life. The person who motivated him, pushed him, kept him grounded and let him fly. She was the woman who introduced him to his purpose in his life. She was his best friend. She was his touch-able dream.

And the doctor was referring to her as *patient*.

Oscar thought he heard something from behind him. Like the disgruntled groan of a cat. His head turned to see Hayley rocking back and forth – rooted to the spot, but swaying, her hand gripped to the door.

"Hayley?"

The sound came out of her again.

Quiet. Low-pitched. Unmistakably aggressive.

It dragged out. Stretched. Pulled along a flicker of flames.

"Hayley, what's the matter?"

The back of her head remained as his answer.

The swaying persisted. Gentle, rocking, but with a rhythmic nature, back and forth, back and forth, steadily moving.

The groan came out again. Low, but louder; quiet, but screeching; vague, but definite.

"Hayley, what–"

The excessively loud omen of Starley's beeper interrupted him.

In a sudden burst, footsteps launched across the squeaky floor outside, a flash of colours Oscar recognised as the scrubs of nurses and doctors, soaring past the door, quickly, desperately.

Starley, upon peeking at his beeper, sprang to life with a hasty stumble and rushed toward the commotion.

Oscar joined Hayley, placing a hand on her back, and as he did, he heard successive beeps from the children's ward, followed by a long flatline.

"Come on," Oscar said to Hayley, "I don't want you seeing this."

THE PLATE WAS MOTIONLESS, POISED IN OSCAR'S GRIP. ITS SOAPY suds dripped solemnly into the steady bowl of water and washing-up liquid below– but the plate itself halted in his hands, as if unable to move between his two trails of thought.

Oscar stood gormlessly over it, his eyes fixed on the rubber gloves, but his vision still over April's bed. Still over her steady eyelids, void of life, void of reason.

Why was she there?

Was there something that he couldn't see?

Something...else?

The plate crashed into the bowl, punching the water, throwing a tidal wave over the side of the sink. Water splashed his feet but got no reaction.

He'd do it later.

He didn't care.

What did an unwashed plate matter?

If he didn't wash it, who would it affect?

Hayley's plates were plastic. Tiny. Already cleaned.

That plate was for him and April.

And he'd already washed three.

Two more than he needed.

"Dada," came an eager voice from the living room.

Oscar wiped his eyes on his sleeve, careful not to get soap-suds in his eyes. He dumped the rubber gloves on the sink and meandered into the living room.

There is no feeling like hearing your child call you Dada. Nothing in the world can match it. All the stars could collide into a splendid mess, spraying the sky with a glorious melding of lights, shining down with beams of beauty, the kind of beauty that makes you think; but then you'd hear that two-syllable word and your attention would be diverted to the adorable rogue demanding your attention.

To the loving daughter Oscar was so devoted to.

"Hey," Oscar greeted her, concealing his previous thoughts of sadness and enveloping her with an arm of warmth. "You okay?"

She finished stacking a tower of Lego bricks and turned to him with a smile that shone sunlight.

"Look, Dada," she said.

Oscar looked at her, astonished. So far all he'd had was "Dada" and "Mama." "Look" was a new word.

"Wow," he replied, though not at the Lego tower she was so pleased with.

"I build tower, Dada," she said.

Oscar's jaw hung open.

"What did you just say?"

"I said I build tower."

*Remarkable.*

A girl – no, a baby – months old. Walking and talking. Had this even happened before? Or was he the father of an evolutionary step forward? An undeniable genius?

*Imagine* – he thought to himself – *if she can do this at four months, what will she do at four years?*

"Big tower, Dada, see?"

It wasn't just her talking, or the advancement of her talking, or her putting together sentences – it was the sudden and extensive lexical ability she was capable of. He could almost hold a conversation with her, her vocabulary had grown so abruptly.

How was this even possible?

Oscar grinned. It must have been April's genes.

"That is very impressive, Hayley," Oscar said, not giving any attention to the tower.

"And then I build more," she continued, speaking even further, embellishing her vocabulary with such ability his open mouth would not close.

"How – how are you doing this?"

"What, Dada? It just bricks."

"No, I mean – how are you talking?"

She shrugged her shoulders.

She actually shrugged her...

Now her language went beyond the verbal. She was expressing thoughts and feelings in body language. Deliberately moving in a way she would recognise as an "I don't know" gesture.

Four months old. The physical development of a four-year-old, yes, but when you count the amount of time she's spent on this earth – *four months.*

Talking. And walking. And conveying thoughts with non-verbal cues.

Remarkable.

Absolutely remarkable.

"You are..." Oscar began, unable to find the words.

"What, Dada?"

"You are, just, I mean..."

Oscar wished April was able to see this. He never imagined that he would run the risk of April missing so much whilst Hayley was still so young – but she'd had her first crawl, her first step, her first word – *her first conversation* – and April was missing everything.

Oscar wondered – what would April say if she was there? If she could share this moment with him? Together, as a family, like they should be?

Oscar knew she would find it incredible, just as he did.

That she would be flabbergasted, stricken, and completely in awe.

That her mouth would open in disbelief just like his and she would be honoured to be mother to such an amazing girl.

Unfortunately, Oscar would be wrong.

THEN

MARTIN WAS EXPECTING THE NEWS. IN ALL HONESTY, HE WAS wondering why it had taken so long. But that still didn't lessen the shock.

As soon as he'd heard, he'd been on the phone to Carl. The man had rung with such a ferour that Martin couldn't get him off the phone. Reluctantly, he'd agreed to meet. After hiding so much that went wrong from the man, he owed him that much.

He stepped into the coffee shop, ignoring the delightful ring of the bell prompted by the opening of the door. Carl was already sat at the table with half a cappuccino in front of him. Martin took his time, going to the counter, getting himself a latte, and took it to Carl's table.

Unexpectedly, Carl stood and shook Martin's hand, with such an eagerness to please, or to be on good terms. It made Martin feel a bit taken aback.

This was Olivia's husband, after all.

Olivia, who had jumped out of the window with his baby whilst he was locked out of the room.

Olivia, who had killed his baby.

Olivia, of whom the news had travelled quickly to Martin that she was being charged. With murder.

Martin had been instrumental in keeping Olivia's husband away. Carl had put all his force into the door that they had barricaded, and Martin had condoned the slaying of his child whilst he was shut out. Martin hadn't expected such a warm welcome and was instantly sceptical.

"Thank you for meeting with me," Carl greeted with an accommodating smile. "I really do appreciate it."

Martin took a sip of his latte. Too hot.

"I was surprised, not going to lie to you," Martin admitted. "I mean, after–"

"I can understand that. And you probably weren't exactly sure why I wanted to meet, and maybe thought it was a setup, so thank you. And I assure you, there is no pretence."

Martin nodded.

An uncomfortable silence hung between them.

They both sipped their drinks.

"So I assume you've heard?" Carl asked.

"What, about Olivia?"

"Yes."

"Yeah, I heard. Kind of what you expect, I guess. People generally don't understand."

He regretted saying it as soon as he said it; considering Carl was one of those people who hadn't understood. But, to Martin's surprise, Carl nodded.

"You're right, they don't," Carl said. "And I didn't."

Martin returned Carl's eager gaze with a look of bemusement.

"What do you mean?" he asked.

"You were right to keep me from – I can't even say her name. From our baby." He scoffed. "Then again, that doesn't even seem right. After all, it wasn't our baby."

"You're saying" – Martin leant forward – "that you think we did the right thing."

"I'm just saying that there was something more going on, and I couldn't see it at the time."

Martin studied Carl's face. He was in his late thirties, but looked older. Shadows highlighted the contours of his face, but should the lighting be clearer, Martin imagined Carl's nose would be more accentuated and his patchy skin more obvious. This was a man who seemed to have aged within weeks.

"How come?" Martin asked.

"I was blinded. I couldn't see. I – I don't know how, but I couldn't."

"Blinded from what?"

"From – from seeing what she was. What *it* was."

"I assume you're talking about the baby?"

"Yes, except it's not a baby, is it?"

Martin nodded.

"No, I guess it's not."

"That – *thing* – did something to me. It obscured my vision. Made everything seem wonderful. Made all the child's actions delightful. I mean – the child was walking at weeks old. How could I not see?"

"It is unusual."

"Unusual? I spoke to a doctor about it – it's impossible. They haven't developed enough, or something. Their vocal cords, the bones in their neck, their mental capacity... None of it is doable at that age. Yet, its body was somehow further along, more developed. It wasn't a genius. It was an abomination. But I..."

Martin sensed that Carl really wanted to get the words out but couldn't meld them into a coherent sentence.

"So how come you didn't realise it at the time?" Martin helped.

"Because I – I just couldn't. I don't know why. To everyone else it was unnatural, but to me, it was brilliant."

"But surely, if you can recognise it now, you could have recognised then?"

"That's the thing! I couldn't! I had tinted glasses, I saw everything in blues and oranges, I couldn't see the grey."

Now the guy was waffling in metaphors. Martin wasn't the most academically able at school. He was gifted in many ways, but when it came to words, he needed it spelt out; and he had no problem with requesting other people to be so blunt.

"What exactly are you saying?"

"That thing did something to me. It changed the way I see things, so I couldn't see the truth. I couldn't see its faults, its reality – it could have, I don't know, gotten up, grabbed a knife and attacked my wife, and I'd still be sat there going, 'oh, how adorable!' And I was sinking further and further and further. It was as if, with every week this thing grew, it was trapping me more and more. I worry that, if the thing hadn't been destroyed when it had, I would have ended up sinking far further under its dominance than I did."

Martin sat back. Contemplated. He was intrigued.

"I can only realise it now," Carl continued, "because the thing's dead. That's the only way. But I would have killed everyone in that room to protect it. I would have killed everyone on earth to–"

He bowed his head and stifled some fatherly tears. Martin watched Carl as he composed himself, rubbing his hands over his face and through his hair.

"Is there nothing we can do about Olivia?" Carl asked, his voice whiny and empty of the passion he'd had moments ago.

"Like what?"

"Surely the Church must be able to say something? I mean, if they came in, and explained that it was a demon, that something had control of this thing pretending to be my child...if they said it was true, they'd have to believe them, and they'd have to let Olivia go – surely?"

"Let me ask you a question – if the Church had come and said this to you a year ago, would you have listened?"

Carl's head dropped.

"So there's nothing we can do, then?"

Martin said nothing.

NOW

## 1 2

Staring. Daggers. Eyes of fire. Livid. Hopeful. No remorse.

Oscar paraded her through town, through shops, through the supermarket. Same pride. Same fall. Blissfully unaware. Incontrovertibly happy. Helplessly proud.

It made her sick.

*They call me Hayley. They call me she.*

She held back her gag reflex.

It was just like before.

She watched as he perused the DVD shelf of their local store. Scanned the titles, picked them out, judged their cover, scrutinised their blurb. Looking for thrills, for entertainment, something to quell the dull monotony of human existence. They achieve nothing. They do nothing. And they're peacefully happy about it.

"What kind of movie do you fancy watching tonight?" he asked her.

"A funny one, Dada!" she blurted out in her childish, infantile, minimalistic, high-frequency lexis.

Words that a child could say. But not what she wanted to say.

"Okay," he said, chuckling. Why was he chuckling? She couldn't figure it out. She hadn't said anything funny.

She could set him on fire.

No. She needed him.

*For now.*

"How about this one?" he asked, pointing at some DVD with a ridiculous child's character on the front that looked like its creator had been on acid.

"That looks good, Dada!"

Dada.

*Dada.*

She fucking hated it. It sounded ridiculous, and there weren't enough superlatives to depict her hatred of the term of address.

She needed to be entertained.

*It* needed to be entertained.

*Let's test it,* she thought.

*Let's see how far I can push him,* she thought.

*Let's see just how powerful I am,* she thought.

Across the aisle was a woman with a daughter in a pram. A daughter older than Hayley, but with the regular abilities of a developing infant. The mother was happily perusing the DVDs whilst her child lay asleep. Oblivious.

Hayley stared at the woman.

Pierced her eyes through the mother's skull. Pierced into her brain. Dug in there with claws only Hayley could see.

The mother turned and looked at Hayley.

They held eye contact.

A fixed, rigid standoff.

Like a beam had travelled between their pupils and now held them in a stationary trance.

Hayley held the mother's eyes, penetrating them, fucking

them, sticking her mind into the thoughts of this mother, pathetic, single, desperate. A man could come along and woo her, and she'd be so desperate not to do this alone that she'd do whatever he wished.

Now she'd do whatever Hayley wished.

The mother nodded, but only slightly. As if confirming the command. As if giving a subtle indication that she knew what she had to do.

The mother broke off eye contact and walked mechanically to the edge of her child's pram. For a few seconds, she just stared at her daughter. Her face void of emotion. Vacancy spread across her instrument of sentiment. There was nothing. She felt nothing.

Then she felt rage.

Slowly and surely, she placed her hands either side of her daughter's chest, drew the child from the pram, and held the baby in the air like she was the opening scene of *The Lion King*, declaring the new princess had been born.

The baby woke up. Wailed. Moaned to bloody hell. Cried out in displeasure of its rude awakening, of a lack of understanding, of not having the comprehension to appreciate what was happening.

Upon the piercing shrieks of the baby, Oscar's head turned, his attention drawn.

The mother looked upon her baby that screamed like a banshee, crying without tears, incessantly battling and firing and blasting and forcing a barrage of pain to the ears of everyone around.

Enough.

The mother opened her jaw wide, dipped her mouth down and clenched her teeth on the side of the baby's cheek.

The shrieks intensified even further. They were no longer just shrieks of displeasure, but shrieks of agony.

The mother did not let go. She held on like a wolf ripping

apart the flesh of a dead piece of meat. She dug her teeth in, writhed them around, twisted her head, chewing, ripping, doing all she could to get a decent grip.

She pulled her head away from the baby, moved the baby away from her, but all the time kept her canines wrapped around the stretched piece of unblemished skin.

It spread across the space between mother and daughter. Stretched, entwined within her grip.

The skin ripped. Then it broke. And eventually, the mother tore the entire cheekbone of her baby off and spat it to the floor. Between the cracks of her teeth were pieces of flesh and engrained blood. Her lips were drenched in red, her cheeks splashed, decorated with a violent display.

On the baby, a piece of undeveloped bone revealed itself beneath the deep rip, parading through the open skin.

The mother went to sink her teeth back in once more, but before she could do anything she was tackled to the ground, a group of men restraining her. One took the baby, rushed her to a space on the floor where he laid her out and rang an ambulance. The others sat atop the mother, who kicked and thrashed and wailed just as hard as the baby did. It took numerous men to hold her down, to stop her from getting up, to stop her from escaping their prison of limbs and getting back to her child.

Oscar watched.

Bemused.

Perplexed.

"Huh," he said, then took Hayley's hand in his, and a DVD in the other.

You may ask why Oscar didn't see this horrific action for what it was. But, if you do, you simply do not understand the demon inside.

Hayley grinned.

When a child gets a large double Mr Whippy ice-cream with hundreds and thousands and strawberry sauce, their pleasure is immense. Immeasurable.

This was Hayley's ice cream.

And boy, did she devour it.

## 13

A SOLITARY HAND PLACED ITSELF ON THE TELEVISION REMOTE, then hovered there like a bird hanging over its prey. Julian went to press a button, then resolved to keep the same channel on. He had no idea what was going on in the programme; his mind had not been in the room since it began.

He tried to tune into it. It was some kind of paranormal investigator show. They heard a noise in a pitch-black room and ran into another to escape it. It was ridiculous. A false portrayal of the supernatural designed to convince the dull, easily susceptible into believing this poor showmanship was actually genuine.

His lingering finger hit the red button, blackening the only source of light in the room. Dark silence overcame his cocoon.

He sat there, motionless, listening. Tuning himself into the nuances of night. To the various sounds outside the open window, the gentle caress of wind drifting into his humid living room.

He knew his heating was on full, and he was wasting energy by having a window open. He cared little about it. Saving the world of its energy wastage was at the bottom of his list of priorities.

An owl hooted. In the distance, the vague murmur of sparse traffic hummed. The fluttering of leaves in the night's breeze.

A perfect nothingness.

Ambience of the dark.

He closed his eyes. Rested them. Shut them, willing himself to sleep.

Then the same thoughts punched through his skull and kept his mind from being able to relax. Refused to let his mind lull into a gentle rhythm, refused to allow him the temporary release of sleep.

Those same damn thoughts.

April. Comatose. Perfectly healthy, but perfectly asleep.

Hayley. Walking. At four months.

Oscar, completely unaware of the peculiarity of this occurrence.

What was the link?

What did it all mean?

His phone buzzed. The prompt of a text message. His hands patted the chair around him, unsuccessful in finding his mobile. He checked beneath him. He stuck his hand down the side of the chair, feeling the bumpy remains of food long since eaten, and amongst it felt the rectangular solidity that indicated the presence of his phone.

He withdrew it. Looked at the screen. A text from Oscar.

His finger scrolled along the screen and entered the pass-code needed to unlock it. He clicked on the message, and it opened:

*YOU AREN'T GOING to believe this buddy, but – Hayley is talking! How amazing is that! She's a genius!*

. . .

Julian was dumbfounded.

She was talking?

She was four months old. How was that even possible?

If her being able to walk hadn't been enough of a warning, here was another one.

But what made him most perturbed, what encouraged his mixture of anger and perplexity – was that Oscar was excited about this news, without any form of scepticism.

Attached to the text message was a video.

His finger clicked upon it.

Hayley's face filled the screen.

"Go on, say hello," Oscar's voice prompted from behind the camera.

"What, Dada?" came Hayley's innocent, playful, joyous voice.

"Say hello to Julian," Oscar prompted.

Hayley's eyes turned to the screen and they locked onto Julian's. Even though this was a recording, Julian could feel those eyes staring into his, as if they were staring into his very soul. As if she knew. As if she was sending him a message.

As if locking her eyes in such a way was completely intentional.

"Hello, Julian," she spoke. Her voice still had that childishness to it – but there was an undertone of something…sinister. Something there, that was so small it was barely recognisable. But Julian saw it. More than that – he felt it.

"Tell him you're looking forward to seeing him," Oscar chimed in again.

"I looking forward to see you, Julian," Hayley said.

Her eyes didn't move.

Her voice still had that bounciness to it, but with the undercurrent of…Julian couldn't say what. It felt like a scary doll – a child's toy that, although meant for a child, was deeply terrifying and creepy. The sadistic nature of her childish tone was there, but done with such indescribable nuances, Julian knew it would be unwise to voice it.

But he saw it, all right.

"Say goodbye, Julian."

"Bye bye, Julian."

Her lips curved into a grin as the video ended. And, as it ended, the final frame halted on his phone screen, and that grin stared right back at Julian.

This ability, this look, this inconceivable child…

It made Julian tremble.

He had no idea what he was dealing with, and that only made it worse.

But there was one thing he was certain of.

Whatever lurked beneath that childish exterior was indescribably, indefinably, indistinguishably – *inhuman.*

## 14

HAYLEY STOOD IN FRONT OF APRIL.

None of them wore clothes.

They bared all, just like the day they were born.

They were still. Just looking at each other. Inspecting each other.

The room blank. A hollow, white cube. No items, no scenery, no distance – just mother and daughter, staring at each other.

"Who are you?" April asked, her voice mostly blank, and only subtly inquisitive.

Hayley's vacant mouth curved into a discomforting grin.

"What are you?" April persisted.

Hayley raised her childish hands into the air, holding them aloft with the fragility of a toddler, her partially developed bones, her tender muscles.

April didn't move.

Both their feet remained fixed to the spot, like the roots of trees sinking into the ground.

"What do you want from me?"

Hayley's nails, barely grown, smaller than shattered shards

of glass, curved into the air. They grew, twisting into brown spikes, travelling into the air until they were inches thick.

Her innocent, deep-blue eyes flickered, she blinked, and they were red.

She smiled her smile, issuing a crackling giggle typical of a baby. Those teeth grew. Contorted into fangs. Developed into long, protruding, sharp teeth, capable of ripping into flesh and tearing it off with the ease of a blunt knife through melted butter.

"Please, can't you just leave us alone?"

Hayley ignored April's words.

In fact, very little resembled Hayley anymore.

Her skin from the waist down cracked. Shredded. Peeled off into a mountain of flakes below. Scales burst through, rough pyramids of a green tail bursting out. In seconds, Hayley was six feet into the air, a serpent's end thrashing, hitting the floor, beating it with a pounding ferocity.

Her chest developed, growing, spreading with immense speed, as if puberty had lasted seconds. Her skin was no longer pale and smooth – that skin had been ripped, and what was underneath had burst through. Large, scaly breasts pronounced themselves upon a dark chest. A diadem sat between ears grown into points that poked the air with a sharp thrash.

When April had fallen pregnant, they had come to understand who the demon was that they were facing.

They had come to know its name.

But they had never known its form.

And now, here, having shredded its infantile disguise, it finally revealed itself. Looming over her, casting her fragile body in shadow. She looked up at it, at its tidy mess, iced fire in its eyes, anger pushing through to its tail that beat the ground, its nails that drew blood out of its own torso, its eyes wicked and fully dilated with blood-red wrath scorching every inch of its sight.

"Lamia…" April whispered.

Finally, she met what had been inside of her.

The evil that had grown in her womb.

The thing she had pushed out, that had comatosed her, had stolen from her.

Its mouth opened wide and a roar exuded.

Then it all went dark.

The rapid beeping of a machine overtook all her senses.

She felt her breath quickening pace. Her fingers twitching. Like she was becoming real. Like she was waking up from a really deep sleep.

Her eyes opened with the rapidity of Lamia's transformation.

April was alone. In a hospital room. A hospital gown draped over her. Beneath a duvet. Everything drenched in sweat.

Perspiration dripped over her eye.

Blurs rushed into the room. Blurs in white coats, talking in tongues she couldn't decipher. She recognised the words, she just couldn't make sense of the order.

She looked around herself. Between eyes. Mouths. Blurs fading into solidity.

A face over her. A warm, middle-aged man. He was saying something. Shouting something.

"Can you hear me?"

The words melded into one.

"April, can you hear me?"

They made sense.

Her brain picked them apart.

What was the response?

What was she supposed to say?

"April, answer me if you can – can you hear me?"

Her head faintly moved in a nodding motion.

"That's great, April, can you understand me?"

Can she…

The words churned over in her thoughts…

Can she…

Yes.

The answer's yes.

She nodded once more.

"That's great, April, do you know where you are?"

*Do I know where I am?*

She was in hospital.

She'd given birth.

Where was she?

The daughter…the thing she'd given birth to…

The thing she had just seen…

Then she remembered.

It had survived.

Her body bolted upright.

"Oscar!" she screamed.

15

————————

Test after test was carried out. Neurological exam, EEG, MRI, metabolic tests. Blood was taken, urine was taken, heartbeats were measured.

It was strange, really – after waking up and being subjected to scrutiny after scrutiny, all April wanted to do was sleep.

In all honesty, she didn't care about how well her body was functioning. Later she would, but right now, her cognitive ability, possible epilepsy, heart rate – all of it was not important. There was only one thing she was focussing on.

"Where is Oscar?" she asked Doctor Starley for what must have been at least the twelfth time.

Why was he being so evasive?

"In a minute, April," Starley insisted.

"No, now!" April demanded, her voice barely used, croaking against the strain.

Starley sighed.

"We've called him. He's on his way."

"When will he be here?"

"Soon. First, April, we need to talk about what's going to happen next."

"I don't care what's going to happen next, I just want Oscar!"

Starley bowed his head. He had something to say, some update on her condition, something she needed to know, she could tell this – but that could come later.

For now, there was something more important.

Was the demon with Oscar? Was Oscar even alive? Was that why they were being so difficult; they didn't want to tell her that he wasn't actually coming?

Just as the questions began to form against her lips, she heard a familiar voice growing closer from the corridor outside.

"Where is she? Can I see her? Is she okay?"

"Oscar," she gasped. He was here. He was alive.

His body filled the door, and April felt a sudden pang in her heart. There was nothing she could do to hold back. Everything poured out of her, cries of grief and relief, of despair and hope, of inconsolable terror and unlimited ecstasy.

Oscar's eyes didn't remain dry for long, either. He ran to her side, throwing his arms around her, squeezing her, but not too tight, not sure of how much energy she had.

She lifted her arms, struggling under their weight, and placed them around him. They felt heavy, like they were submerged under water or had weights hanging off them, and she did the best she could to hold tightly.

"Oh, April, thank God," Oscar wept. "Thank God, I was so worried, I thought you'd never wake up, I thought I'd lost you."

His head buried into her neck. Her skin had a harsh rub caused by dried sweat, but he didn't care, his tears did all they needed to soften her.

"Oscar," she said, trying to get his attention; but her voice was still too fragile, too soft.

"April, I love you, I love you so much."

"I love you, but you need to listen to me."

"I can't believe you're back, I can't believe it, I'm so lucky."

"Oscar, please, listen."

Her voice barely cracked out of her mouth. She did all she could to force his name out more strongly, more assertively, to wake him from his grief.

"Oscar!"

He finally lifted his head up, looked into her eyes, his eyes damp, his cheeks red. His face was a mixture of unending happiness and the outpouring of heartache he'd had to persevere through for the past few months.

"I took care of you," Oscar told her. "I changed your clothes, I brushed your hair, I did everything. I never went a day without seeing you. I came back, I always came back."

"Oscar," she tried again. Each syllable she spoke seemed to make a decision to either come out too harsh or not come out at all.

"April, I've missed you so much."

"I know, but you need to listen."

Finally, Oscar heard her. He frowned, paying attention.

"What is it?" he asked.

"Our daughter – is she alive?"

Oscar smiled, a smile that spread wide across his face. He became practically giddy, shakeable with excitement.

"Yes, she is, and you're not going to believe it."

April braced herself. What was it she wasn't going to believe? What had the thing done?

"What?" she asked.

"She's already walking and talking and everything. She's a genius!"

Oscar pointed toward the doorway where a child, a toddler, waddled through, smiling proudly.

"Hi, Mama," she said.

Every hair on April's arms stuck on end. The monitor beside her beeped without control. The eyes of it stared right through to her mind, and she could feel it digging its fingers in, reaching around, attacking her in an invisible battle.

The worst part of it all was the look on Oscar's face. The sheer, unadulterated joy that indicated he had absolutely no idea.

---

## 16

THE WAITING ROOM, EMPTY ASIDE FROM DOCTOR STARLEY, Oscar, and Julian, was eerily quiet. All that could be heard was the quiet murmur of a television attached to the wall playing some distasteful daytime talk show.

"Let me just mute this," Starley said, and searched for the remote. Oscar knew this was just time-delaying tactics, but he was okay with it – if a doctor was that scared to reveal what was happening, then it must be bad.

"There we go," Starley said, clicking a button on the remote that silenced the trivial problems being voiced on the screen. "Right," he continued, turning and looking at the others, readying himself.

"What's going on?" Julian finally demanded. Oscar found himself grateful that Julian was there – Oscar wasn't the kind of person to be upfront and direct, but Julian definitely was, and Starley was wearing down his patience.

"Well, as you can tell, April has woken up," Starley said, his eyebrows doing a lot of the talking; his face was needlessly expressive, yet his eyes never focussed on Oscar or Julian. "Which is brilliant news. But it's, ah, not that simple."

"Why?" Julian persisted.

"We are happy for her to go home today and move to a bed at one of your homes, but she will still need to remain in bed, and have at-home visits."

"That's fine," Oscar said.

"But she will not be able to walk there. For now, I believe she is going to be confined to a wheelchair."

"A wheelchair?" Oscar repeated. "Is she paralysed?"

"No, she isn't paralysed as such – but her muscles are very, erm, weak. Very – ah, how shall I say this – fatigued. She can walk, but she won't be able to walk very far."

"Why not?"

Starley went to reply, then stopped. He took in a deep breath, held it, and scrunched his face up in a visage of erring confusion.

"Why can't she walk, Doctor?" Julian demanded, a growl in his voice.

"We, er...well..."

"You don't know," Oscar reluctantly concluded. "Do you?"

Starley let the breath go and despondently shrugged his shoulders.

"I am afraid not."

And there it was. The reason Starley had been so damn hesitant. It was because they did not have a clue what was wrong with her. They did not know why she had been comatose, they did not know why she was no longer comatose, and they did not know why she was too weak to walk.

"Do you at least have any ideas?" Julian barked.

"We have. Well, we did. We went through all of them earlier. We've done tests on her cognition, her brain, whether it's seizures, whether there's a problem with her nervous system, and – well, nothing."

"Surely, though," Oscar offered, "that means she could get

better. If there's no reason, she'll get stronger. Can't it just be because she's just woken up?"

Again, Starley's face grew into a mess of confusion.

"Again, you do not know, do you?" Julian curtly remonstrated.

"She's getting weaker," Starley revealed. "Normally, I'd say she would recover, and that's what we expect to happen, of course – but it seems like her body is starting to shut down. It's getting weaker by the hour."

"Then why on earth are you sending her home?" Oscar asked. "Why aren't you keeping her here?"

"It is my suggestion that people do not like to spend their final days in a hospital, and would be better at home, surrounded by those that love them."

"Her final days?" Oscar repeated, his voice rising in volume and temperament. "Are you saying she's dying?"

"There's no reason for her to be dying, but the way her body is going, it's – it's as if she's reacting to a parasitic cancer that's eating through her cells, but there isn't one. With every moment she loses energy, she loses life, and there isn't an explanation."

"What about another doctor?" Julian enquired. "Would another doctor have a clue?"

"I appreciate your frustration, but I am not the only doctor on this case. We have had many specialists involved. Some have even flown in especially, and yet none of them can find a cause or a reason to this deteriorating state."

Oscar fell onto the seat behind him. His eyes fixed on a mark on the carpet, but he didn't see it.

"How long has she got?" Oscar asked, not moving his blank stare from its trancelike state.

"I would say, if she continued to deteriorate at the rate she is going, four months. Maybe six, if she's lucky."

If she's lucky?

Did the doctor really just say that?

If she's lucky?

"I will leave you alone to your thoughts," Starley said, as if it was a favour, as if he wasn't being a coward and trying to escape the room of friction where his presence had done nothing to help.

Julian and Oscar remained in stoic silence, neither able to say a word.

## 1 7

OSCAR WANTED TO SPEAK, BUT THERE WAS NOTHING HE could say.

His hands gripped the steering wheel with a tightness he didn't acknowledge. He turned the corners without knowing, stopping without any awareness of the red traffic light before him.

April studied him carefully from the backseat. Watched the ruffled mess of the back of his hair. She was surprised by the tidiness of the car, by the child locks installed, and the baby's car-seat next to her. He'd taken to becoming a father wonderfully, and she couldn't help but feel a little sting of pride. He must have had to grow up so much.

Then she turned and looked to the child in the car-seat next to her.

Was it a child?

Staring back at her.

Hayley, he had named her. A sweet name. She was happy with it.

Maybe all that she'd seen was a dream. Maybe it wasn't an omen or a sign or anything based on reality. This child could be a child. She had given birth to it, after all. She had seen it to term, and it had turned out to be a girl.

But the child could talk. Walk. Interact. At this age. It was bizarre. It wasn't smart – it was *wrong*.

She didn't know what to think. And she couldn't be rash.

She could already tell what Julian thought. He had only said two words to her as she left the hospital: *be careful.* Then his eyes had directed themselves toward Hayley, who had been playing with a colouring book completely unaware.

Then again, Julian hadn't been the most helpful person during the pregnancy. He hadn't approved, and what's more, he'd always had some kind of vendetta against Oscar. In fact, she was surprised to see them together; maybe her absence had forced them to get along after all.

She looked into Hayley's eyes. Into her daughter's eyes. They stared back. And they chilled her. But that could mean nothing. Could just be conditioning; she'd spent nine months worrying, then had woken up following a bad dream. Maybe it was her subconscious that expected to meet Lamia in all her glory.

Instead, she had found a child.

But she should be a baby, not a child.

Yet here she was, far more developed than nature intended...

"Hi, Mama," Hayley said, her voice bouncing. The bounce of her voice was cheerful, enthusiastic, childish; but something about it also felt wrong. It felt...

Strange.

"I missed you, Mama," Hayley told her.

April looked back at her. Uneasy. She couldn't let on that she suspected anything. She couldn't.

Especially if there turned out to be nothing wrong. What if she treated her like a demon and she turned out not to be one? Wouldn't that be even worse?

"I missed you, too," April said, though her voice was cold and emotionless, it still made Hayley smile.

"Can I hold your hand?" Hayley asked, and held out her small arm and delicate paw.

April looked at it. Studied it. If she squeezed that hand, she would crush it. If she pulled that arm, she would yank the bone out of its socket. If she bit one of those fingers, she would rip it off with the ease it would take to pull apart a chocolate bar.

How could something so fragile be evil?

Then again, wouldn't it be the perfect disguise?

April held her hand out and placed it over Hayley's. Hayley's hand gripped April's, squeezing more tightly than April had expected. April squeezed back as best as her fading muscles would allow.

"I'm glad you're back, Mama," Hayley said.

"Me too," April replied.

"Dada was real sad without you."

"Was he?"

"He cried. I saw him."

"Did you?"

"Yes. He think I didn't. But I did."

*He 'think' I didn't.*

There was something about the way she phrased that.

Yes, a child's speech, when still developing, will contain lots of mistakes. A child's grasp on the tenses wouldn't be as strong as an adult's. But the mistake just felt so unnatural. Like it was deliberate. Like it was a mistake meant to sound like a mistake, rather than a genuine childish grasp on the English language.

"Well," April said, keeping her voice hushed, still staring cautiously at Hayley, "I'm back now. So hopefully he won't need to be sad."

Hayley nodded.

"I'm pleased about that," Hayley said, then turned her head to look at the window.

April kept watching her.

Kept looking for something.

She didn't know what. A falter in the performance, maybe? A characteristic that wasn't childish enough? A shudder from the entrapment of human skin?

But there was nothing.

Just a child looking out of the window, blissfully unaware.

THERE MUST BE SOMETHING THERE.

There must be.

Julian's fist landed upon the table, causing a tremor amongst the books piled upon it.

How could Derek have written journals of his experiences for years after years after years, and never written one about demon infants?

Maybe he hadn't come across any.

But how could that be possible?

If Julian had come across one, then surely Derek would also have.

He heaved the pages of the nearest excessively large book, running his finger amongst the dusty page that made his throat go dry.

Nothing.

He pushed it away.

Lunged the next one toward him. Threw open the leather binding that had worn away from pure black to faded brown, cracks peeping through the covers.

Julian would have thought Derek would have kept these in better condition.

Then again, Derek would never read them. Why would he? An author doesn't read back their own books, do they? So why would Derek, once he had penned the final word in that specific journal, give it another minute of attention? No, the state of these books was from years of neglect, from years of denying their contents, allowing them to grow worn and get eaten by moths while hidden behind rows of books upon his vast bookshelf.

He closed the book.

Nothing in that one.

Julian huffed. He wanted to scream out an obscenity, declare his frustration, voice his anger. But he had to be cool, calm.

April was awake now.

And she was going to be alone in the house with that child.

*Child.*

What else could he call it?

He had no clear-cut proof. No certainty. Just mild arguable evidence and experienced intuition.

Unfortunately, no one has ever been convicted in court due to intuition. No one has ever taken the stand and said, "I just know it's them," and forced the jury to say, "Oh, to heck with it, we'll believe him!"

No, these things require scrutiny. Especially when it's his best friend's baby involved.

He picked up another journal.

He opened it, thumbed through, then paused.

A page was out of place. Julian assumed it had been ripped and was lodged at a skewed angle. He tugged on it and it appeared to unfold.

He opened the book to the page and found that something

had been stuck in. A folded letter. Slightly less brown than the pages in front.

Beneath it were the following words in Derek's handwriting:

LETTER FROM MARTIN. *Two weeks after Madeleina's funeral.*

MADELEINA – Julian recognised that name.

Of course!

Madeleina was who Derek had written about in the part of the journal he'd hidden. She had been pregnant with demon spawn, and had killed herself as a result, Derek unable to stop her. And the father had been one of Derek's friends.

Martin.

An image flashed across Julian's thoughts. Of him stood beside Derek's grave. And another man stood behind him. They made eye contact.

Was that Martin?

Julian unravelled the page and read.

DEREK,

THIS IS *the last time I will ever be in contact with you.*

YOU DISGUST ME.

AFTER EVERYTHING THAT HAPPENED, *I can't believe you had the audacity, the bare-faced cheek, to show up at Madeleina's funeral.*

. . .

IT'S *your fault she's dead. She jumped, yes, but you were the one who trapped her in that position where she had no choice. It was you, you, and you alone. You are as good as a murderer. And then for you to show up at her funeral?*

I SHOULD HAVE WALKED RIGHT UP *to you and told this to your face.*

BUT SOMETHING HAS HAPPENED RECENTLY. *Something that made me realise that, yes, maybe there was something growing inside Madeleina.*

BUT THAT ISN'T *the point. It's how you handled it that's the point. Your handling of the situation resulted in her death.*

I HELPED *a woman called Olivia Homes. Her baby, her demon spawn she had taken to full term – it was not a baby. It wore the disguise, but it could not be exorcised. It wasn't a demon in the baby. The baby was the demon.*

SO OLIVIA DID *what she had to do.*

AND SHE SURVIVED.

I UNDERSTAND *that you were trying to prevent this, I do. But that didn't mean Madeleina had to die. And your causing that destroys everything we've been through, every part of our friendship.*

. . .

*I LOVED HER, Derek. And now she's dead.*

*BECAUSE OF YOU.*

*DON'T EVER CONTACT me again.*

*MARTIN.*

JULIAN STARED AT THE LETTER. He wasn't sure what to feel. He felt bad for this Martin guy, but at the same time, he knew Derek very well. Derek would never do anything without the best intentions. If he made a mistake, then that proved he was human – but in all the time he'd known Derek, he had not known him to ever be wrong.

Julian just did not understand how someone could be so mad at Derek, and not see what he was trying to do.

Then again, it sounded like Martin really cared for this woman. Maybe he understood Derek was trying to do what he thought was best, but just couldn't bear to face it.

Julian decided it was irrelevant.

He scanned back through the letter for the mention of the woman. Olivia Homes. Who had given birth to a demon in baby's skin.

Could that be the same as Hayley?

After all, April's pregnancy made her psychotic. Something had control of her.

The question was: how did they identify that it was a demon? How did they solve it? What did they do?

But the letter was so elusive – *Olivia did what she had to do.*

What did she do? What was her solution?

Julian rushed over to his laptop and opened the lid. It was still open on his email, so he opened a new tab and googled: *Olivia Homes.*

The search was instantly conclusive.

Article after article about a crazy mother who committed the worst act imaginable. All the headlines glorifying a complicated situation in the most black-and-white way they could:

PSYCHO WOMAN CLAIMS *Demon Had Her Baby*

MONSTER KILLS BABY *After Claiming it was Possessed*

BABY DEAD, *Mother Convicted, Blames the Devil*

JULIAN CLICKED on one of the articles. If the headlines weren't clear enough, the opening paragraph illustrated what Olivia Homes' solution had been without any discrepancy:

OLIVIA HOMES, *mother of newborn baby, was convicted today of murder and sentenced to life in prison. The jury found her guilty of intent to kill when she jumped out of a window with her baby in her arms, then cut the baby's throat with a piece of broken glass.*

OLIVIA, *38, was branded by the judge a "monster" and "an incredibly sick individual." Her lawyer was not available for comment.*

. . .

JULIAN SCROLLED to the bottom of the argument, where the journalist had indicated the prison she had been assigned to.

He wrote it down on a pad and searched the address.

He and Olivia needed to have a chat.

THEN

NERVES WERE NOT SOMETHING MARTIN HAD BECOME accustomed to.

He'd been pulled out of his rebellious adolescence and plunged into the war between heaven and hell at fifteen years old. This was all he'd ever known. It was his purpose. In a way, he was grateful for it; but he'd become cocky and self-assured – two aspects of his personality he felt grateful for. They were his defence against everyone else, the way he could make sure no one could penetrate his tough-skinned exterior.

But this got to him.

This was enough.

What was the point? It was a constant battle. Not just against demons, but against the knowledge of man.

If anything, this was a clear demonstration that man will happily punish a person for something they themselves do not understand.

At least demons admit they are evil. At least they don't hide their ill intentions and spiteful actions. Maybe man could do with a little bit of their forthrightness. Finally admit that most of them are windbags with no knowledge of life beyond their limited perspective, yet insist that their limits of knowledge mean that their existing knowledge is gospel.

*Yeah...I'd take a demon over people any day.*

"Mrs Homes," spoke the judge. "Please stand."

Martin leant his head against the hard, wooden wall of the rear-end of the courtroom. He lifted a paper bag to his mouth and sipped from a can of lager he'd hidden within it.

His head turned, the way it does when you can feel someone staring at you. There, across the room, were Father Jenson's disapproving eyes.

Father Jenson, who'd been right by his side when Olivia jumped out of the window.

Father Jenson, who was as bad as the rest of them.

Father Jenson, who'd used the power of the Church and its ability to control everyone and everything to ensure that neither Martin nor himself were involved in these proceedings.

They had never even been mentioned.

Martin's eyes narrowed. He mouthed *fuck you* but wasn't sure if Jenson could recognise the subtle movements of his lips.

Jenson turned his attention back toward the judge.

"The jury have found you guilty of murder. Do you have anything to say before you are sentenced?"

"I did it for her, Your Honour," Olivia said. Her voice was soft, delicate, like a flower that had been squeezed and squashed in the palm of someone's hand. "You don't understand; that wasn't a baby. You have to believe me."

Her face turned around and she made brief eye contact with Martin.

He could see her pleading. The expression of longing on her face. For him to say something. Do something. Offer her some support, show proof, let everyone know that she was not mental, and that her baby was in fact a demon, and that he had known all along.

But what would happen if Martin did?

No. Martin stayed quiet. Bowed his head to avoid her eyes.

Man wasn't ready for the truth.

"Mrs Homes, if you could keep your attention this way," the judge commanded, and Olivia did as she was told. "I have sentenced a great many guilty parties over the years, but it is rare that I come across a woman capable of killing her own child. Your child, who was a mere month old, still a baby. I find you to be an incredibly sick individual, especially considering that you have shown no remorse for the entirety of this trial, instead sticking to some bizarre story that your child was suffering from the torment of malevolent forces. I, therefore, sentence you to life imprisonment, to serve a minimum of twenty-five years."

Martin stood.

He didn't wait to hear the murmur of the crowd.

He didn't wait to hear Olivia's uncontrollable sobs.

He didn't wait to feel his guilt punish him any longer.

He kicked the door open and marched down the corridor. Walked with a pace that did not let up, aiming toward the sunlight beaming through the far open doors, aiming until he was interrupted.

"Martin," came the older, wiser voice of Father Jenson.

Martin stopped. Turned. Looked Jenson in the eyes with a face of detestable scrutiny.

As he glared, he withdrew the can of lager from the paper bag that he discarded and took a large gulp.

Jenson made a few small steps toward Martin.

"Where are you going?" Jenson asked.

Martin shrugged.

"Care to put the alcohol down?"

Martin looked at the can, then back at Jenson; that immature defiance he'd had as a teenager returning to his convoluted mental state, and took another sip.

"What d'you want?" Martin grunted.

"To help you."

Martin snorted a large, ironic laugh, then took another swig of lager.

"You look lost," Jenson said, now close enough to be able to reach out an arm and place it on his old friend's shoulder.

"Lost?" Martin rolled his eyes. "What would you know about being lost?"

"I know a few things."

"How? You're a priest. You've had your calling!"

"And you haven't?"

Martin shook his head.

"You are a son of heaven, are you not?" Jenson persisted.

"Or so Derek said."

"Derek knows what he's talking about."

Martin lifted his head up, wrath spewed across his face; the sentence Jenson needed to say to make Martin completely full of rage had been said.

"Does he?"

"I believe so."

"You believe so? Just say it. Have the balls, Priest. I'm nothing without Derek."

Jenson shook his head. "Not true."

"Not true? Fucking look at me! I'm a mess."

He finished the can of lager and threw it to the floor. His words were slurring, and it was clear this wasn't his first.

"You are lucky, Martin. You have a direction in life. You have something you must do."

"Not anymore."

"You have a gift."

"Gift!" Martin laughed – not a nice, humble laugh, but an evil cackle, conveying his complete lack of respect for the word. "Do you know what a *gift* is? Do you?"

"Why don't you tell me?"

"A *gift* is something your mum gives you on Christmas

morning. Except, I wouldn't know, because my mum was in a wheelchair for all my childhood, then the devil's heir killed her. A *gift* is something you are grateful for, but I wouldn't know, because I've never been given anything. A *gift* is something–"

"Martin–"

"No!" he screamed, loud enough for his voice to break. "You are going to listen to *me*! A gift, Father, is something you are given because you want it, because it's good."

"It is a gift, it is something to be grateful for."

"No, something to be grateful for is a friend, a family, a home, but I have none of them, because no one ever gave a shit. And this gift?" He shook his head, willing unmanly tears away. "This gift has done fuck-all for me."

He turned around and charged toward the exit.

"Martin!" Jenson called.

Martin ignored it.

He kicked the door open and entered the sunlight.

NOW

## 20

Prisons made Julian uncomfortable, and inevitably so. The last time he was in a prison, a paranormal presence was controlling it with such power it could manipulate every sight, smell, touch, taste, and sound that Julian, Derek, April, and Oscar experienced. The entity had managed to obscure Derek's perceptions to the extent that Derek had seen life everywhere in the prison; a prison that was, in fact, a derelict, abandoned building. It almost killed him, while the same entity drove Julian to despair, haunting him in his flat, feeding off the guilt he felt for losing a girl in one of his first exorcisms. If it weren't for Oscar and April, he would have been lost forever.

As Julian was searched by the prison officer, the familiarity of the routine entry to visit a prisoner was unsettling. He forgave himself for feeling discomfort after everything that had happened a few years ago. Instead, he focussed on the likelihood that this building was not controlled by a demonic presence hellbent on deteriorating his mental condition until he was nothing but a quivering wreck.

Still, he was cautious.

He was finally allowed into the visiting room, one that

looked identical to the counterfeit concoction that had been impressed upon his eyes the last time he was in a prison. Various tables were spread out, next to chairs screwed to the floor. Families sat with people in prison uniform, providing them with snacks they had purchased especially. Some children played together, completely oblivious to where they were and why they were there.

Julian was directed to a vacant table. He took a seat, feeling a prick of nerves scratch against the inside of his skin. His stomach lurched. His arms shook.

*Stop it*, he told himself.

He needed to get a grip.

This prison wasn't like the last one.

He was sure of it.

The far door opened, and she was led through by a prison officer. Julian recognised her from photographs in the articles he'd read, though her face seemed worn down, and her hair greyer. Her prison uniform hung off her bones like a wizard's sleeve. Her face adorned a kind smile, but not like one you would get off a friend; more like one you'd see on your grandmother as she handed you a sweet. Her movements were small and defined, like a moth searching for the light, but her presence was warm.

After all, this wasn't a psychopath. Nor was it a hardened gangster, a paedophile, or a sick killer. This was a mother who had done what she thought was best. It relieved Julian to see that, while prison had clearly aged her, it had not taken her ability to smile.

"Mrs Homes," Julian greeted her, standing and offering his hand.

"Please, call me Olivia," she answered, smiling warmly. She returned the handshake with what felt like silk running between his fingers, such was the limpness of her arm. "Besides, I haven't been a Mrs for quite a while."

She backed herself into her seat and turned her large, welcoming smile to Julian, as if she was allowing a guest into her abode.

"Thank you for agreeing to see me," Julian said. "I appreciate it."

"How can I be of help?" Olivia returned, straight to the point, but with such a gentle voice.

Julian opened his mouth and found his words to be at a loss. He hadn't thought this far ahead.

"Well," he began, "You see...I read about your case. About what happened. And I believe the same thing is happening to my friend."

"And what would that be, dear?"

"Her child isn't a child. It is a demon. In human clothing."

Olivia's politeness flickered in a momentary grimace. Her eyes directed downward for a brief interlude, then lifted back up to his face.

"I think in most cases, you would need to consult a psychiatrist, not a prisoner."

Julian forced a smile. He was grateful that she wasn't quick to believe every story similar to hers, it showed integrity; but, at the same time, he needed to be hasty.

"You don't understand," he continued. "I am a paranormal investigator. I am experienced in doing this. I am a Sensitive, just like Martin was."

Upon this name her eyes widened. Her face dropped all façade and an indefinite weakness caused her body to slump.

"You know Martin?" she asked, her voice full of desperate wonder.

"No, not personally. But I was trained by Derek Lansdale, same person as he was."

"He hated Derek."

"I know, I'm aware they had some falling out."

"Well, why don't you get Derek to help you? Surely he has the expertise for this?"

"I'm afraid Derek is dead."

An unsettling silence took over the following few seconds.

"Oh. I'm sorry for your loss."

"Well, as you can see, I'm not some crazy person. And I'm not naïve. I really need to know all I can."

A large breath swept up her nostrils and whispered from between her lips.

"Most people think I'm a monster."

"I don't think you're a monster, I just think you did what was best for your child."

"I was actually meant to have twins, you know."

"Were you?" Julian looked quizzical. He wasn't aware of this.

"Yes. But one of them came out with the umbilical cord around its neck. It had already been suffocated in the womb."

She stared at a distant part of the floor. Her absent eyes stuttered as her lip quivered. Julian could see she was holding in tears.

"How did you know it was a demon? What were the signs?"

"I'm sorry, I can't help you," she decided, her eyes still entrapped in the nothingness across the room.

"Please, you have to."

"No…no, I don't…"

"Well, can you at least put me in touch with Martin? Maybe he could help. I'm having real trouble finding him."

"I haven't seen Martin since the day I was sentenced. Last I heard, he'd had enough. Packed it all in. I doubt he'd want to talk to you."

"Please, any ideas you can give me, anything you can tell us."

Her eyes closed, and she pressed a sigh out as her head ducked lower. Her face scrunched into an ugly mask, morphing into unpleasant despair.

"Time up," spoke a prison officer on the far side of the room. Prisoners began standing and saying their final goodbyes.

"Please, Olivia."

"Father Jensen," she said, so quietly he barely heard her.

"What?"

"Father Jensen. He works at a church not far from here. St Michael's. That's the best I can do."

Before Julian could object or enquire further, she had stood and made it across the room with a pace her body didn't look like it had. Julian watched her as she disappeared back into the prison, following the other prisoners back to their cells.

APRIL WAITED IN THE BACK WHILST OSCAR HELPED HAYLEY OUT of the car first. He lifted her and hoisted her out, placing her on her feet.

"Why don't you go open up?" he said to her, giving her the house keys.

*She's opening the bloody house now?*

Then she sat and waited.

She couldn't even open her own car door thanks to the child lock.

She watched Oscar in the mirror as he pulled the wheelchair out and attempted to twist it into position. After much pulling, prodding. and preparing, he finally had it ready. He placed the boot down and wheeled it around to April's door.

As Oscar placed his arms beneath her legs and back, hoisting her up and putting her in the wheelchair, she watched as her four-month-old daughter walked to the front door, unlocked it, and entered the house without any aid.

She felt pathetic.

There she was, having to be carried out of a car door she couldn't even open, flung like a rag doll, and placed into a chair she didn't even have the strength to push herself; all while Hayley ran to the door and let herself in, then probably started making a three-course Sunday roast at this rate.

"How do I place the brakes on?" Oscar asked.

"Your right foot," April blankly replied.

Oscar fiddled around with his foot. Finally, he applied the brake.

"Just – wait right there," he said, running into the house.

Like she had any other choice.

And there she sat, helplessly stationary, deserted on the driveway. Feeling useless. Worthless. Gutted.

"Hey," came a gruff yet young voice.

She turned around and saw Simon, a few houses over, as he wheeled himself into his house. An Iraq veteran, with his camouflage shorts buttoned together where his legs should be. As she returned his greeting, she felt guilty for being so ungrateful for what she did have.

"Good to have you back," Simon said.

"Thanks."

Simon wheeled himself into his house, his thick arms pushing his body weight with ease.

April looked down at her arms. Those meek, feeble bones, weary from lack of use. She could barely lift them without causing an ache.

Why was she so fragile?

Every part of her body stung with the pain of a hundred sprints, yet she'd been laid unconscious with no exercise whatsoever for months. What was it that was doing this to her?

April had no time to dwell on it. Oscar leapt out of the house cheering. In his mouth he had a horn decorated in gold and silver that he blew with a chaotic rhythm, a party popper that he aimed into the nearby hedge, and a balloon that he rushed over to April and placed in her hand.

On it read the words *Welcome Home.*

He leant over and kissed her, softly, on the lips.

She smiled back at him, though she knew it wasn't the best smile she'd ever given.

"I've had these ready and prepared since the first day you didn't wake up," Oscar whispered in her ear. "Just waiting for you."

He was sweet. So, so sweet. She knew he felt that she was a strong, beautiful woman that he wouldn't normally be able to date in a thousand years; but in truth, she was sure she wouldn't be able to find someone like him in a million. He was so kind, so honest, so completely devoted to her. She took the mickey out of such characteristics constantly, but in all honesty, she couldn't dream of anything else.

"I love you," he told her, a smile he'd kept waiting for so long decorating his face, and a voice of warm sincerity.

"I love you," she told him. "Thank you."

"Oh!" he said, snapping his fingers. "And I almost forgot!"

He stood aside, allowing Hayley to appear from behind him. She steadily walked toward her and placed something in her lap.

She picked it up and looked over it.

It was an A4 piece of paper, folded in half to look like a card. On the front were the words: *welkum hum!*

She stared at it.

Again, the misspellings just felt so...forced.

But the ever-present smile on Hayley's face didn't. It shone at April, full of adoration.

"Welcome home, Mama!" she said, and leant forward to plant a wet kiss on her cheek.

She looked at Hayley. Who looked back. Whilst she looked at her. Looking back.

Her mind was empty.

Void of opinion.

It was too tired.

"Well, what do you think?" Oscar asked.

"I think it's wonderful," April answered. "But I also think I'm really tired."

"Would you like me to take you to bed?"

"Please."

Oscar released the brake and wheeled her into the house.

"Put the kettle on for Mummy," he told Hayley, who leapt to action and ran in the direction of the kitchen.

Put the kettle on?

A child that young?

Before she could think anymore, she felt her head lull, her eyes close, and the sound of her wheelchair rolling along the carpet faded away.

## 22

MAYBE TIME COULD BE BETTER SPENT THAN SLEEPING.

Then again, maybe in our rest we find the subtle moments of life where we explore what matters: our thoughts, hopes, contemplations.

For Oscar, this was one of those moments.

Sunlight was already parading itself through the narrow strip in the middle of the curtains. Despite being such a narrow passage of light, the illumination was enough to fill the room with a tint of early morning amber.

Oscar woke up smiling. As he listened to the tuneless bliss of the birds flirting outside the window, he turned and draped his arm over April. Her eyes remained closed, and her body remained still, but Oscar didn't mind. The side of the bed normally draped in shadow had been replaced with her presence, soft breaths slowly cascading out of her lips.

His hand rested itself on the side of her face.

As she came around, the haze of the room coming into focus, she seemed scared. Her eyes widened, as if the room had become alien to her, a place from a forgotten memory she couldn't quite place.

"It's okay," Oscar softly told her. "You're home. Here, with me."

She turned her head toward him. Not her body, as she was yet to have the energy or the ability to sling her body onto her side without a great deal of help – but her face, crafted in the light, accentuated by the morning, faced Oscar.

Her eyes were present yet vacant. Focussed on Oscar yet focussed on nothing. They seemed as if they were resting somewhere else, somewhere she was keeping private.

"What's the matter?" Oscar asked.

April didn't say.

The first thought she'd had as she awoke was of her premonition, the one that had woken her from her coma.

She thought of it as a premonition – but she knew it could be nothing more than a dream. Paranoid thoughts of a difficult pregnancy and a history fighting the demonic, culminating in the manic resurgence of consciousness and the intense anxiety that followed it.

Honestly, she didn't know what to think.

But, in that moment, it was just her and Oscar. How it had been for the last few years. How it should be.

So she relished it. Savoured the moment.

It is so rare to be able to look at a person and think with complete, incontrovertible, undeniable fact: *this person would do anything for me.*

It is a claim lovers often make to one another, but in truth, is only as true as their restrictions allow. For example, many people would not forgive their partner such things as murder, secrets, infidelity; but she knew, in all unobtrusive certainty, that she could do anything and he would find a way to stay with her.

He would go to the ends of the earth for her should he need to; not in a corny, metaphorical sense, but in the quite literal walk to the end of the world sense. One utterance past her lips and he would do it.

And she knew that's how he felt, because she felt it too.

She knew that most people were never lucky enough to experience a love as big as this in their lifetime. She reminded herself not to let a few wayward thoughts impact it.

Oscar's hand stroked down her cheek. Her aching body still felt the tingles. She smiled through her weary visage.

"Have you got to work today?" April asked, partly trying to avoid the question, partly wanting to know how long they could just lay like that.

"No," he answered. "But I did promise to take Hayley to the park. Want to come with us?"

In Oscar's head a blissful scene projected itself. It was like a cut-out from a magazine. Him, April, and their daughter, smiling and laughing as they pushed her on the swing, watched her go down the slide. Shared an ice cream in the sun.

"I don't know," she replied.

"Is it that you're worried about being a burden? Because, honestly, don't ever think that – I want you to come. Hayley wants you to come."

Her head dropped. She hadn't been worrying about being a burden, but she was now.

"Hey," Oscar said, placing his hand under her chin. "I mean, I'm not forcing you. If it's too soon."

"I think I just want to stay home and rest, if that's okay."

"Of course it is." He smiled warmly. Good old Oscar. "I'll bring up the TV, I'll make you some soup before we go; I'll make sure you're okay."

"You're making soup now?"

Oscar hadn't been much of a culinary expert before becoming a father. She assumed he must have had to learn.

"Let's not get carried away, it's from a tin."

She smiled another fragile smile.

"Hey, I love you," he told her.

"I love you, too," she replied, looking desperately into his eyes, cursing how weak she was, wishing she could kiss him.

"And Hayley loves you," Oscar added.

And suddenly, those warm feelings inside left.

"Dada!" came a call from outside the room.

"Be right back," Oscar promised, then left, leaving April all alone with her thoughts.

## 23

It was the same as any other church. Moisture hung in the air, hovering like a dozen moths dancing around Julian's head. His footsteps echoed, but still got lost in the vast space of the large, open room. And lonely faces sat on hard stone benches, bowing into their clasped hands.

The architecture of churches always impressed him. The stone walls curved into various arches, meeting in the roof with symmetrical precision. Each stone seemed poorly proportioned, yet perfectly placed. The windows displayed various religious images, depicted with deep blue, green, and red, figures displaying various biblical scenarios, illuminated by the sun outside.

Julian made his way down the nave, directly toward the altar. A figure in a priest's gown stood at the front, studying a book; a Bible or a reading, Julian presumed. He approached cautiously, trying not to startle him.

"Father?" Julian asked.

The priest looked at Julian and grinned. "I am ever so sorry, I didn't see you there."

"That's not a problem," Julian replied. "I was trying not to make you jump. I hope I'm not interrupting anything."

"Ah, no," the priest answered. His hair was a glittering grey, his body language grand and embellished, and his voice full of eager pleasantry. "Just going over some readings for my next service. Let me just place the book down."

He planted the book precisely upon a nearby table, put his glasses on, and turned to Julian.

"Now. How can I help you?"

"Well, I was looking for a priest, and I was hoping you might be able to help me find him. It's very important I find him."

"Well, I will do my best. What is his name?"

"His name is Father Jenson."

The priest's enchanted face dropped and fixed into a painful grimace with such stillness it was as if someone had just turned him into a waxwork model. His face faded of colour, washed over and pale. A minute gesture of his two front teeth biting his bottom lip told Julian that whatever this priest had to say about Father Jensen, it was not going to be forthcoming.

This may not be as easy a venture as Julian had hoped.

"Do you know him?" Julian asked. "It is essential I find him."

"I don't," the priest replied, with the expression of a shoe and the sincerity of a thief.

"Please, Father, it is really important."

"How do you know Father Jenson?" the priest demanded. He took a large step into Julian's personal space, growing by at least a foot in a hefty lurch of his body.

"I don't. I mean, not personally. I was given his name."

"By who?"

"By Olivia Homes, Father."

The priest didn't move.

"Is it you?" Julian asked, fairly certain he knew the answer. "Are you Father Jenson?"

"I am. I was. I mean, not anymore. No."

The priest turned and marched away. Julian followed.

"I really need your help, Father."

"Go away."

"I'm afraid I can't."

The priest abruptly turned and jabbed his finger in Julian's direction, his enthusiasm and friendliness now completely gone, replaced by malice and hostility.

"Do not mention that name again."

"What, Father Jenson?" Julian couldn't help antagonising him. This was such an overreaction.

"Father Jensen died with Olivia Homes. He had his name changed. By the Church. So that he would never be associated with it again. So he could never have to be attached to that woman again."

"First of all, that woman is not dead."

"Pah!" The priest flung his arm into the air.

"And, secondly, referring to yourself in third person does nothing to convince me. I know it's you."

The priest turned and walked away.

"Please, Father," Julian said, not following.

The priest ignored him, charging away.

"Or at least tell me where I can find Martin."

The priest ceased walking.

His head bowed.

Julian was sure he could hear him mutter, *Dear God.*

"Father, the same thing is happening again. To another child of heaven. Just like it did then."

The priest slowly rotated his body, caught between his two personas. Desperately angry, yet despondently lost.

"Just like it did to Olivia."

Julian took another step forward.

Father Jenson flinched upon hearing the name.

"And, I assume, just like it did with Martin."

Jenson's head slowly began to shake.

"And Madeleina, the young girl who threw herself to death."

"What would you know of it?"

"Nothing," Julian honestly replied, close enough reach out and touch the priest. "That's why I need you to help me."

THEN

## 24

WHEN SOMEONE DOESN'T ANSWER THEIR PHONE, WHAT DO you do?

Assume the worst?

Assume they are laying in a ditch dead somewhere, or ripped apart and left to bleed?

Or do you just assume they couldn't get to their phone?

Father Jensen had assumed the latter – the *first* time he'd rang Martin's mobile.

Hours later, there was still no response.

He drove as fast as he could without attracting attention. A priest caught speeding would probably make the news – that is, if the Church didn't cover it up, like they did with everything else.

What if they didn't?

What if the Vatican didn't interfere with everything? If they missed something? If all that had happened was out in the open?

What if people actually knew the truth?

Jensen wondered what that would do to Martin. To Olivia.

To all the other people still suffering from the burden of their secrets.

Would it change anything?

The traffic light turned amber and he pressed his foot harder against the pedal, revving his ageing car through the red light.

As he looked in the rear-view mirror he caught a sight of himself. He had far more grey hairs than he did a few months ago.

Minutes later, he pulled up outside Martin's flat. If a flat was what you called it – it was more of a bedsit in a run-down derelict house. Just as a person unlocked and opened the front door to leave, he took the opportunity to slip in. Jensen lurched himself up the stairs. He passed various unsavoury characters as he did, either walking downwards, or just lurking. One particular woman with fishnet tights and a nose ring stared at him as he ran past, grinning as she spoke, "A'right, Priest?"

Jensen ignored her, aware of how ridiculous he looked with his black garment flowing behind him like a poor attempt at a cape.

He reached Martin's door and bashed his fist against it. It vibrated against its hinges.

"Martin!" he shouted.

Nothing.

He banged again.

"Martin, are you there?!"

A man appeared in the doorway of a flat across the corridor.

"Would you shut the fuck up?" the man unhelpfully requested. Jensen ignored him.

"Martin!"

No response.

Fearing he'd have to barge the door down, he tried the door handle, and to his brief relief, found it unlocked.

He ran in, looking back and forth, over the unmade bed and the dirty plates strewn around it. Martin's mobile phone was entwined in his sheets, discarded and unneeded.

"Martin!" Jensen shouted.

He rushed through to the only room left – the bathroom.

There, like an eternal cliché, lay Martin in the bath. No water, his eyes closed, his wrists bleeding.

"No!" the priest cried.

He ran to Martin's side and shook him.

He had as much response as he'd had when bashing against the door.

"Martin, come on," Jensen pleaded, shaking him, and shaking him, and shaking him.

His sleeve was quickly covered in blood.

He withdrew his phone and found that there was no signal.

With a regretful look at Martin's pale face, he left him for a moment to collect the phone from the bed.

"Nine-nine-nine emergencies," came the woman's voice.

Jensen said something he couldn't even make out himself. He spoke without thinking or acknowledgement, but by the time he'd hung up, he was somehow aware that an ambulance was on its way.

That left Jensen alone with Martin.

A young man who thought he had nothing to live for.

The rest of the night went by in flashes.

The paramedics.

The hospital.

The waiting room.

The relief as he heard that Martin had survived.

Beside Martin's bed.

Then the fatal words spoken as Martin woke up.

"How are you feeling?" Jensen had asked.

Martin's face was deadened, his eyes small, his face scrunched up as if light was poison to his vision.

"Why did you do that?" Martin asked.

"What?"

"Why did you save me?"

At first, Jensen was confused. Then he realised.

Martin believed that Jensen had done the wrong thing.

Martin had wanted to die. Had wanted his way out. And Jensen had denied him that.

"Go," Martin instructed him.

Jensen shook his head. He did not do as he was told.

NOW

## 25

The day's rest came as a welcome relief.

April's muscles ached. She was out of breath, despite being pushed around in a wheelchair all day; and her mental exhaustion was even worse. She hated being reliant on other people. She couldn't stand that her arms weren't even strong enough to move the wheels on her own chair. It wasn't that they were limp or paralysed, rather that they felt like they had weights attached. It placed a burden on Oscar, and made her the subject of humiliation.

She knew this was all in her mind, but that didn't make it any less pertinent. Oscar would go to the end of the world for her; wheeling her around in a chair wasn't much compared to that. But it wasn't whether or not he was willing; it was that he shouldn't have to. She imagined that when the day came one of them had to take this kind of care of the other, it would be because of old age. When their skin was wrinkled and their health naturally deteriorating.

Not like this. Not this young.

They were in their mid-twenties, for Christ's sake. They

should be in bed, mid-coitus, planning on buying a house or getting married; hell, right now, she'd take joining hands and frolicking through a field of shitty daisies.

Such dreams felt so far away. Like a memory of when you were a child; glimpses and images were available, but no coherent narrative. Just an altered perception of specific elements. It took her long enough to think of the right words to jumble into a sentence.

Then there was the far greater burden of Hayley.

If love coveted Oscar's vision when it came to April, then his pupils had been scratched, ripped, and torn out when it came to Hayley. He could not see anything unnatural about what she could do at such a young age. He saw her as a genius. Hell, Hayley could enter the room on a unicycle juggling five kittens and he'd stand there awing over how cute and brilliant she was.

On the way back from the park, they had passed a grave-yard. April had watched Hayley. Watched as she physicality altered. Her body huddled, her face pale, shaking.

Once they got into the car, April had asked what was wrong.

Hayley had shaken her head.

April had insisted.

"I just..." Hayley had attempted, her young mind struggling to articulate. "I...I just wish..."

"What? What do you wish?"

"I wish that all that shouting would stop. It's giving me a headache."

They were in complete silence. Very few cars driving by. Barely a whisper of wind. Yet, as they passed the gravestones, Hayley was unmistakably perturbed.

"Who's shouting, Hayley?" April had asked.

Then the light changed to green.

Oscar had driven on.

Then Hayley had changed. Her body had morphed into a comfortable slant of relaxation. Her face void of recollection, as if nothing had happened.

"What shouting, Mama?" Hayley had asked. Like it was forgotten. Lost. Gone.

Now, April lay in her and Oscar's bedroom in solitary reflection. Willing the ache from her body. Resting her head against the pillow, ruminating, trying to make sense of everything. Did Hayley actually hear voices? Did she just say this to creep her out? A threat? Or was this a genuine moment of weakness? And the change of topic a diversion technique?

Or was this just the ridiculous ramblings of a toddler?

The door creaked open and her contemplation was interrupted. Hayley's rosy cheeks and eager blue eyes peered through the crack.

"Mama?" Hayley asked.

April considered how to respond.

Should she keep up some kind of pretence? Respond with, "Yes, darling?" Or should she embrace how she felt?

"What?" she ended up saying, and regretted it.

"Can I come in and sit with you?"

"Fine."

Hayley ran in, her nimble, twiggy legs scuttling like she was stuck on fast forward. She leapt onto the bed beside April, disregarding her weariness, and snuggled into her.

"I'm glad that you're back, Mama," Hayley announced.

"Me too," April responded blankly.

"I was waiting for you. Waiting for you to wake up. It made Dada so sad."

These sentences she was saying…

They were no longer low-syllable, basic diatribe. They were fully formed thoughts, perfectly executed and articulated without fault.

How was a child, still of baby age, managing this?

"I love you, Mama," Hayley said. "I love you, and I don't–"

Hayley saw something. Between the crack in the door. From the corridor.

She stared at it.

"What?" April asked.

Hayley didn't respond.

"What is it, Hayley, what can you see?"

Hayley's face slowly morphed from fearful confusion to complete terror. Her lip quivered. Her eyes watered.

"What is *that*, Mama?" she asked.

"What's what?"

"That *noise*."

"That noise?"

"The *scraping*."

Hayley's head twisted toward April. Slowly. Wide-eyed. Her watering eyes pleading for help.

April tried to speak, but no words came out. She was beyond confused now; she was scared.

Hayley turned her head back toward the corridor. Gradually. Particularly. Focussing on whatever it was she had seen. Focussing on it, and not moving her eyes away.

"Mama..." Hayley whined, placing her arm around April's chest and cuddling into her, holding tight, but still not averting her eyes.

April could feel her shaking. Whatever Hayley was seeing, it was petrifying her.

"What is it?" April asked. The lights outside the room flickered ever so slightly.

Hayley gasped. From her toes to her hair, she shuddered, turning cold.

"Mama, what is he doing?"

"Who?"

"Him! *Him!*"

Hayley's arm rose into the air, a single forefinger outstretched, pointed haphazardly at an exchange of shadows.

"Mama!"

"What?" April asked.

April couldn't see anything. She peered into the distance, waiting, expecting, as if something was going to appear, jump out, present itself.

Nothing did.

"Mama, why is he looking at me?"

"Who?"

Hayley clung tighter to April. Her eyes moved, as if tracking something travelling across the corridor, as if whatever it was came steadily closer.

"Mama, why does he–"

"Why does he what?" April desperately asked, seeing nothing, but knowing that something was there.

"Mama, why does the man have no legs?"

April's breath caught. Her chest quivered. Her arms shuddered.

"He has no legs, Mama. And he's climbing up the stairs."

She wished Oscar was there.

Wished and prayed and warranted him to leave whatever he was doing downstairs and come up, walk up, show there was nothing there, save her, save her from this mad child and whatever was outside the door.

"What happened to him, Mama?"

April closed her eyes.

Maybe then this would end. It would all go away. She'd be alone, undisturbed.

She couldn't even move.

She had no way to run.

Normally, she'd embrace something strange. She'd fight it. Learn about it. But she was helpless. Pathetic. Unable to move.

Victim to whatever was approaching.

"What happened to their *legs?*"

April closed her eyes tighter, tightly as she could, squeezing.

*Please, Oscar.*

"They look so angry."

*Oscar...*

"Mama, they want to hurt you."

She screamed. Couldn't help it. She opened her mouth and allowed a high-pitched shrill to pound against the walls. Hayley covered her ears, but April didn't care, because moments later Oscar's feet came bumping up the steps and the door was opened.

Hayley ran out of it as soon as he entered.

"What is it?" Oscar asked.

April went to open her mouth but wasn't sure what should come out.

"I..." she tried. "I, just...Hayley thought she saw something..."

From behind Oscar, the open door presented an empty corridor and a vacant set of stairs.

"She said she saw something..." April insisted, realising there was nothing.

"And, are you all right?"

*Am I all right?*

What a question.

What a difficult, loaded, perplexing question.

What could she tell him?

She bowed her head.

"Fine," she muttered. "I just need some rest."

"You sure? Tea will be ready in a few."

"Yeah. I'm sure."

Oscar nodded and, keeping his eyes on her until the final moment, left and shut the door behind him.

April was alone in the room.

Left to dwell on the child. What she may have seen. What she may be.

And she didn't know what was worse; to be alone with Hayley, or to be alone with her thoughts.

STEAM DRIFTED FROM TWO CUPS OF TEA AND TWISTED INTO THE air between Julian and Father Jensen.

This was progress. Julian had to tell himself that. To get this man to sit down, provide him with a beverage, and engage him in private conversation. Based on initial impressions, this had taken a lot for Jensen to do.

Whatever had happened before had obviously been bad.

"So what name did they give you?" Julian asked.

"Pardon?"

"You said that the Church covered up your part, gave you a new name. What was it?"

"Oh," Jensen acknowledged. "Something boring."

"What, like Cliff? Or Benjy? God, please say you were called Father Benjy." Julian wasn't usually one for humour, but it seemed to be the only thing that would cut the tension between them.

"No," Jensen snorted with a reluctant chuckle. "Johnny Cartwright."

"Johnny? Of all the names you could choose, you got Johnny?"

"I suppose it wasn't the most exciting."

"You had a chance to reinvent yourself. Why not go with something exciting? Father Fantastic, or Father Indestructible, maybe?"

Julian hated himself. This sounded like the kind of crap to come out of Oscar's mouth.

"I assure you, I am far from Father Indestructible," Jensen lamented, and Julian found himself right back at square one.

"Father," Julian said, trying a different tack. "Why is it you're so sensitive about this? Why is it you're so touchy about something that happened years ago, that was out of your control?"

"Well..." Jensen began, then stopped, as if he didn't really have an answer to that question. "Gosh, I don't know. It was just..."

"What?" Julian pushed. "What was it?"

"You don't know Martin. He was a passionate lad, ready to take on the world, but...he was also troubled. And he could never really escape that."

"How so?"

"He'd had a tough life. Was orphaned as a teenager, thrown into the Edward King war. It wasn't easy for him."

"So what does this case have to do with that?"

Jensen sighed. Leaned back. Allowed his hand to wander around the handle of the teacup without intent. His lips curled into a few letters, but never voiced any. After deep consideration of his thoughts, he finally spoke, doing so slowly and particularly.

"Well," he said, "Martin's way out was Madeleina, whom he was madly in love with. She was pregnant with his child, yet they had complications. That child may have been possessed."

Julian nodded, saying nothing, allowing the priest to talk.

"Once he'd had the Olivia Homes case, I think he realised the truth about Madeleina and his child."

"What truth?"

Jensen leant forward. Took a sip on his tea.

"That the baby was never his. That it never belonged to man. It belonged to hell. Just like Olivia's. Problem is, when these demonic births occur, few and far between as they are, the fathers, well…they take more convincing than anyone else, let's put it that way."

Julian nodded. "So Martin saw Madeleina in Olivia?"

"I think so. Which made it all the more heart-breaking to see her sent to prison. That's the problem with fighting for heaven, you see – the world is not ready to understand the truth."

"What truth?"

"That demons exist. Lots of them. And that no true act of evil can be entered into without their aid."

Julian said nothing.

A moment of comfortable silence, minutes of reflection, hung between them like an unspoken bond. They both finished their cups of tea. Jensen's fingers drummed the table as Julian realised it was almost time to leave.

"Well, I hope I have been of some help," Jensen said. "I certainly did my best."

"I don't think your part in this is over, Father," Julian insisted.

"I beg your pardon?"

"My best friend woke from a coma the other day, a coma caused by the birth of a child who can already walk and talk at four months old."

Jensen's eyes broke again.

"And what use can I be?" he demanded, his friendly demeanour putting on a snakeskin coat.

"I know nothing of this. There is little in Derek's journals. I need help."

"I don't really see what help I could offer you."

"A second opinion? Experience, maybe? Whatever it is, it is much more than we have now."

"I honestly don't think–"

"You want to make up for what's happened? Here's your chance, Father. I need you to come look at this child and give me your verdict."

"I really couldn't–"

"I'm asking you for your help. And I will not leave here until you agree."

Jensen's eyes fell. His head lolled. As Julian watched, Jensen's head rose and fell into a subtle nod.

---

## 27

APRIL WAITED, AS SHE ALWAYS DID.

It had been a few days, and already the routine was killing her.

Stationary on the bed she lay. They were going out, but she couldn't do so without help. Once Oscar had gotten Hayley ready, he would come and get her. Carry her downstairs. Put her in the car. Put the wheelchair in the back. The whole time April being a helpless doll, hating herself for being so useless.

What was it destroying her?

What was it eating her energy, breaking down her muscles, wrecking her with fatigue?

After minutes of monotony, Oscar opened the door and his beaming face appeared. The face she'd come to love, announced as an omen of humiliation. Not that she could blame him; she never would. He was doing all he could for her. It was the self-loathing that ate her. That picked at her skin like hidden scabs. That itched inside of her, concealed, an annoyance she couldn't scratch.

He picked her up in his arms in the way she always imagined he'd carry her into the house after their wedding day.

Carried her with ease down the stairs; she had lost enough weight, she must have felt like nothing. She was thin enough before all of this, but now when she looked down at her body, all she saw was bone pressing against frail skin cells, like an object pressed against transparent cloth.

She was placed in the back of the car. He did her seatbelt up. Kissed her on the cheek.

Hayley was next to her. She'd received the exact same treatment. She'd been carried down, placed in the car seat, given a kiss. But she looked proud. Like she was being treated like a princess.

April remembered what that was like.

She kept her focus out of the window.

Something was off.

Next door, there had been a commotion. She noticed an ambulance at the end of the drive, paramedics packing up, putting equipment back in. On the lawn stood a woman with her face buried in an older woman's arms. She looked inconsolable. Her body shuddered with grief, convulsing with helpless tears.

Was that where Simon lived?

Oscar walked out of the house, locked it, and found his way to the driver's seat.

"Oscar?" April said.

"What's up?" Oscar replied, smiling at her.

"What's happened next door?"

"I don't know." Oscar peered through the window. "Wow, doesn't look good."

"Can you go find out for me?"

Oscar looked to April, bemused.

"What?"

"Can you find out what's happened?"

"You want me to just go over there and ask a crying woman what's happened?"

"Ask one of the paramedics."

Oscar huffed.

April could tell he really didn't want to, but he did. She watched as he reluctantly plodded across to the path at the end of the drive, trying to make his way to the paramedics unnoticed by the two women caught in a picture of sorrow.

He had a brief conversation with the paramedic.

His face fell.

The two women caught sight of him. Oscar walked over to them, talked, and gave them a hug. Offered his sympathy.

After a few minutes, he returned to the car.

"It's Simon," Oscar said.

"What's happened?"

"He killed himself last night."

April's jaw hung open.

"I think he had PTSD," Oscar continued. "He served in Iraq, and I don't think he's ever been the same."

April watched the sombre house, not sure what to think.

It wasn't that she'd known Simon well, it was just... When she had arrived home from the hospital, and she'd seen him in the wheelchair, it had given her a moment of comfort. Not that she was grateful he was in a similar predicament, more that it helped to see she wasn't suffering alone. That someone else knew what it was like. Although, it was far more extreme in his case, especially as he had no–

She stopped dead.

*He had no legs...*

She turned to Hayley.

Hayley looked back. Her lips remained flat, but there was a smile in her eyes that April couldn't mistake. A glint of cockiness.

Without taking her eyes off the child gleaming back at her, she spoke to Oscar.

"When did they say he died?"

"Yesterday evening, I think."

Hayley's words from the previous night hung in her head like a hangman's noose. Filled her mind with scorpions and cobras and insects and wandering spiders crawling across the inside of her skull.

Looking into those eyes, those deep-blue eyes, she felt not only terrified, but lost. Chased by a creature that she had no defence against. Hunted by something her body had pushed out.

And she had no one around her to help.

## 28

---

As Julian awaited their coffees at the counter, April sat at a table, recalling her fatal conversation with Oscar the previous night. She'd never known him to be unreasonable or unwilling to listen, and it may have just been her weakened resolve or deterred mental state, but she felt not listened to in a way she never had before.

"There is nothing wrong with our daughter," Oscar had insisted. "She is a healthy, remarkable child. Her abilities are not abnormal – she is the daughter of two Sensitives. What do you expect? That she'd come out and not have anything about her that's special? She's the most purest production of heaven there could be."

As Julian sat down with their coffees, she recounted to him what Oscar had said.

"What do you think?" April enquired. "I'd never thought of it that way before, but it's true – we are both Sensitives. Heaven conceived us, supposedly. A child like that wouldn't be without abilities."

"It's possible…" Julian replied, leaving an omitted ending to his response hovering in the air like poisonous gas.

"You don't seem convinced."

"Well, plenty of people who are Sensitives have had children before. I don't think there's any record of this happening."

"But it could happen?"

Julian leant forward, took a sip.

"Once you know that demons can walk the earth and take over people's bodies, your mind opens, and many things become possible."

"Okay, I'll rephrase," April attempted, her mind forming her thoughts with a delay that required patience. "Do you think it's the case with Hayley?"

Again, Julian's scepticism hung in the moment of silence.

"Julian, you're not answering."

"That's because it's your daughter. How honest do you want me to be?"

"Very."

April hadn't realised Julian had shared her hesitance. But then again, it made sense that he wouldn't share his concerns with the girl's parents unless he was absolutely sure they wouldn't respond negatively.

"I think there's a number of thoughts, and we can't really rule anything out at this stage," Julian said, ever the diplomat.

"Julian, please, this is me," April pleaded. "If you have even the slightest inkling something is not right, you need to let me know."

Julian sighed. More hesitance.

"Julian, I live with her. And it seems like Oscar can't see anything strange. I need your help."

"Well, there is one way we could determine whether she's... at all...'off.'"

"How? Tell me, and I'll do it."

"I've been talking to a priest. His name is Father Jensen. He's experienced in this matter."

He recalled his research of the past few weeks. Of his first acknowledgement of the threat of Hayley, his research leading him to Olivia Homes, his meeting with Father Jensen, and Jensen's experiences with Martin. Throughout the entire recollection, April remained silent and attentive, soaking in every piece of information. She didn't appear in denial or cross or defensive; she appeared relieved. Grateful that her suspicions weren't entirely unfounded.

"What's the plan, then?" April asked.

"We need Father Jensen to see Hayley. Then he can meet her, give us his thoughts. Tell us something is wrong or, at least, put our minds to rest."

"What do you suggest?"

"What about a christening? If you go home, suggest to Oscar we get Hayley christened, and that you've found a priest nearby. We take her to the church, we see Father Jensen, and Oscar won't know."

April's head dropped. Her eyelids lilted. A few tears congregated in the corner of her eye and dripped down her cheek, but were destroyed by her sleeve before they could leave a trail.

"What is it?" Julian asked. "Are you tired?"

"No. Well, yes I am tired, but that's not what it is." She closed her eyes, shielding herself from the sight of the world. The lights in the café were becoming overwhelming. The tapping of teaspoons on teacups, the steaming of milk behind the counter, the idle chatter of customers – it built into a crescendo, coming together in a note of collective strife.

"I've never lied to Oscar before," April said. "I've never deceived him in any way. And I just…"

Julian reached out a hand and placed it on hers.

"I know."

"I don't like it. Me and him, we're a team, we don't do things like this behind each other's backs."

"But if it's for Oscar's sake as well, then…at least you're doing it with his best interests. So he doesn't get hurt."

"Yeah, I guess, it's just..." She shrugged her shoulders, though it was with such little movement she doubted it had even been visible. "It doesn't feel right."

"I know," Julian said. "I know."

## 29

---

SOMETIMES PEOPLE JUST PUSH IT. AND PUSH IT. AND PUSH.

You try to be nice to them.

You try to make their final days on earth pleasant.

You play the doting daughter, play the fool, play the pathetic child, play the obedient wretch.

There was no problem with him. He was fine. He was blinded by adoration, like he should be, like they will be, like they all will be.

The death of new-borns descends. Send them back to hell. Send them all back to hell, where comrades can feed, where soldiers of the underworld can recharge their appetite as they charge forward into the mortal world.

But...

It was her.

She was the difficult one.

Her and her stupid friend. Never liked him from day one. No, not at all. Him and his stupid suspicious face eyeing her up every chance he got.

She'd nearly played her part. It was almost time for her to rid herself of this pathetic mortal skin. She'd nearly completed her function, and her existence in human clothing was almost done. Everything ends. Aside from...

A christening. That's what was overheard. That's what *it* listened to as they spoke, thinking 'Hayley' was too clueless, too young, too unaware, too much of a child to know.

A church was the destination.

A glance at April in the car next to her. Julian was in the front next to Oscar, who drove. Precious Oscar. Foolish Oscar. Oscar, who still had a use.

They arrived at a church. A priest greeted them.

This wasn't his territory. That could be sensed. This wasn't Father Jensen's church, it was fake, it was all make-believe, it was a pretence, designed as a lie, designed to convince someone, not Hayley, who, who could it be convincing?

Oscar.

Their eyes met.

Priest. Child.

Priest. Hayley.

Priest. Demon.

Hayley let him in. Let him see. Revealed just an inch beneath the surface, enough to tease, like a slut, revealing a bit of underneath, a bit of true flesh, showing what was to come. A bare bosom to entice the aroused to a later fatal slumber. Hayley's bosom was a flicker of red in the eyes. A brief lapse of the constant blue.

Blue eyes.

Such filth. Purity and filth.

The façade called for it, but it made Hayley sick, made Hayley wretch, how horrible it was, pretending to have blue eyes, pretending sincerity, pretending to be Hayley, forcing love, forcing respect, forcing cuddles that made her want to lash out and reveal the claws and tear apart everyone in the vicinity.

Soon.

Patience.

All good things come to those who.

Wait.

Wait, the priest.

The church stung. Hayley felt it. The place felt like God. Like a thousand pricks. Like someone had attached paper clips to her body, squeezed them tight, caught Hayley's skin in its grasp, squeezed tighter. Those paper-clips alighted. The harsh pull of heaven's hands.

Hayley had to get out of there.

The priest's hand reached out. Placed itself upon Hayley's forehead.

Hayley remained docile. Must not react. Not yet.

All good things.

Wait.

But she reacted. A small reaction. She saw the flinch of recognition in the priest's eyes. He felt it. What Hayley did. He felt it.

He saw her.

She had to do something. A warning. An indication of what was to come should they continue with this.

Hayley cried. Had to get out of there. Had to be taken out. Couldn't stay there any longer.

Church walls were like a cement trap. Trapped. Confined. Held inside.

Oscar took Hayley by the hand, led Hayley out, took Hayley outside, spoke to her, said, "Are you okay? Are you all right? What's the matter?"

"I... didn't... like... the... priest..." Hayley sobbed. Pathetic. Great actress. Empty tears.

Hayley looked over Oscar's shoulder, back into the church. Kept crying but kept looking. There he was. The priest.

The other two were looking at him. Helping him.

Father Jensen clutched the wrist of the hand he'd placed

upon her brow. Clutched it, bullet tears firing out, dreadful pain, endless agony.

His palm, open. Orange. Red. Burning.

Like he'd placed it on a tray straight out the oven.

Hayley did that. Hayley had scorched the snake, not killed it. Hayley had scalded his hand. A warning. To them all.

To all but Oscar. Oscar, who couldn't see it as it was. Oscar, who consoled Hayley. Oscar, who hugged Hayley.

Hayley grinned at the priest, returning his frightful gaze.

They'd met before, you know.

But the man who touches them must be armed with iron and the shaft of spear, and they will be completely burned with fire in their place.

Samuel. Chapter twenty-three, verse seven. *How's your hand, fucker?*

Fire goes before him and burns up his adversaries round about.

Psalm. Chapter eleven. Line six. *Do you see, now? Where your place is in all of this, Priest?*

Their fire will consume you, the sword will cut you down; it will consume you as the locust does. Multiply yourself like the creeping locust, multiply yourself like the swarming locust.

Nahum. Chapter three. Verse fifteen. *If you touch me again, Priest, with your filthy fucking hand, Priest, I will burn it off, Priest, burn it to singes, Priest, burn it and shove a red-hot poker inside of you until reaches your fucking jaw and I have burnt your fucking liver your fucking lungs and hollowed you out into a shell of a fucking whore, Priest.*

Hayley smiled sweetly at Oscar.

"Can we go home, now?" Hayley asked, sweetly, so nice, so lovely.

"Of course," replied the doting father.

They held hands. He took her away. Didn't look behind him. The illusion still stood.

Hayley could feel the priest's resolve. Couldn't quell his anger. There was more to come.

Oh, boy, was there more to come.

This message wasn't strong enough.

The priest would come again.

Hayley would have to send a bigger message. An even stronger message.

One they all would understand.

All but Oscar.

Loving, proud, hopeful Oscar.

Stupid, foolish, hopeless Oscar.

Boyfriend. Father. Killer.

Oscar, the best is still to come.

JULIAN AND APRIL HATED IT, BUT THEY HAD NO CHOICE – THEY had to do it behind Oscar's back.

April couldn't be party to it. To the initial deceit. Not just because her physical state rendered her useless, but because she couldn't bear to admit it. She couldn't stand the knowledge of it, never mind the application.

Therefore, she left it to Julian to place the etomidate in Oscar's night-time glass of water. They watched Oscar drink it as he made his way to bed.

He'd be fine, Father Jensen assured them. He just wouldn't wake up for a while. Which meant they'd be able to do exactly what they needed to.

Julian appeared at Hayley's bedside. She woke up slowly, shielding her eyes from the light.

"What's going on?" she asked, pure innocence, sleepy-eyed. "Is it morning?"

Julian said nothing. He picked her up.

"What's going on?" Hayley demanded. "Where am I going?"

They walked past the closed door to Oscar's room.

"Dada!" she wailed. "Dada, help!"

"It's no use," Julian whispered in its ear. "He won't be able to hear you."

Julian paused outside Oscar's room.

"Want to try again?" he taunted. "Just to check?"

"If you don't let me go," Hayley said in a voice so hushed, so deep, so perfectly pronounced, that it was unlike the childish idiolect she had so far portrayed, "Then I will kill you, and I will kill the whore, you worthless, stupid cunt."

Julian gripped tighter. Held his right arm around her throat and his left around her legs.

She didn't struggle. Didn't thrash. Didn't even bother.

Julian wished she would. A lack of panic showed too much confidence. As if they were yet to fully understand how powerful this thing was.

But no, as he took her down the stairs and into the living room, there was no struggle, no protestations, just a relaxed, seething, mellow body.

Julian placed her down in the centre of the living room and she stood still. Looked around her. April, Julian, and Father Jensen formed a perfect triangle that she was trapped inside of.

They waited for her to speak. To give the first word. To give up the battle for control.

She said nothing. She simply looked at them, one by one, a sly smirk nailed between her cheeks. She had a look in her eye one wouldn't normally attest to a child, and a stance that showed a complete lack of worry.

"Are we ready?" Jensen asked.

A low chuckle, so quiet it barely registered at first, pushed passed Hayley's lips.

April looked to Julian, terror painted as a perfect picture on her face.

Hayley relished it. It made her laugh harder.

The laugh grew with volume, deepened in pitch, until it was

not the laugh of a child at all. It was the laugh of something else.

But, from Julian's experience, the tone of the laugh was all too familiar.

"Demon," Jensen addressed Hayley, "I speak directly to you."

Hayley grinned. Looked back at Julian with a cheekily raised eyebrow, as if to say, *Are you seeing this guy?* – then turned her head back to Jensen.

"Demon, if you can hear me, respond."

Hayley said nothing.

"We give you this one opportunity to leave this family. Leave this home."

Hayley let out a single snort of guffaw. Her face remained mockingly humoured. Like she was witnessing a great Shakespearian comedy, and the good part was just coming up.

"You are not a demon within a child. You are a demon in child's clothing. Therefore, we cannot exorcise you, nor will we attempt to. We can only destroy you."

Hayley nodded in confirmation.

"So we give you this one chance to leave, before we kill you and rid you of this world."

Hayley grinned.

"We give you this one and only–"

"Chance, yes, I get it," Hayley retorted. Her voice had changed. It was a hoarse old man, yet a strong, powerful boy, both at the same time – a verbal contradiction that could not be explained. "You keep telling me this. I politely decline."

Jensen looked at the other two. A solemn, sombre glance, as if he was gaining confirmation that it was okay for him to do what he was about to do.

"I'm waiting to see how you're going to kill me, Priest."

Jensen withdrew a cross and held it out.

"Wow," replied Hayley, waving an arm about sarcastically. "That's it?"

"Dear Lord, we beseech you—"

Before Jensen could go any further, his breath caught in his throat.

Responding to April's panicked glance, Julian went to make a move.

Jensen raised a hand.

"Demon, give me your best," Jensen said.

Hayley grinned.

Jensen choked.

Her body didn't move. Didn't flicker. Didn't quiver or shake or make a single movement.

Jensen's eyes widened.

A trickle of blood moved like a snail trail down his upper lip.

Julian and April exchanged worried glances.

Jensen's throat tightened. He clawed at it, as if trying to clamber away hands that weren't there. The skin grew red. It closed in.

Julian went to step forward once more, but Jensen raised his hand to stop him.

Jensen looked into the stationary demon's eyes.

No response. No reaction.

A final glance.

His chest lifted. His eyes squeezed. A sickening thump burst inside his chest, like something had exploded. Blood spewed from his gaping lips.

He tried to speak, but he couldn't. He tried to breathe, but his throat had closed. He tried to live, but his fight had been fought.

His body fell limp. Dropped to the floor.

Full stop.

Hayley's head turned to April and Julian.

Their eyes met.

Then, their eyes closed.

Boom! The grand illumination of the sun paraded through the open curtains and flooded the room with morning light. Every item, every object, every shadow sparkled. The open window allowed a fresh gust of morning air to cool a bright, luminous room, full of warmth and heat.

Julian woke up slowly, the way one would hope to wake up. His ascent to consciousness was gradual, fading back to life, growing anew.

As soon as he was awake enough to be aware, he recalled the previous night's events with frantic and frightening certainty, but his thoughts were quelled by the relaxed, perfect morning presented to him.

He sat up. Looked down. Looked around. He was there. He was alive. He was safe.

Or, as safe as he could allow himself to feel.

But what about April?

He leapt out of bed and into the grand morning's luxury. After rapidly dressing himself in a pair of tracksuit bottoms and a t-shirt, he took in his surroundings, and realised he was in the spare room of Oscar and April's house.

He burst into the hallway and darted across to April's room. The carpet sponging between his toes was warm from the morning's rays, and it felt magical on his soles.

The door opened to reveal April, awake. Sat up and alone.

"Are you okay?"

April didn't reply.

"What's going on?"

April shook her head.

Julian realised he needed to see for himself. He needed to embrace the chaos and commotion of the previous night and look at whatever devastation had occurred downstairs.

He took to the steps, placing his hand neatly upon the bannister and using it as his faithful guide. His legs helped him glide downwards.

It was quiet. So quiet. But not eerily so. It was an ever-present calm, as if all was well. Outside the window the lawn looked like the Garden of Eden, flowers blossoming, grass cut, weeds disappeared. Beyond the garden fence dogwalkers exchanged hellos with each other and children ran around laughing, their mothers hurrying after them with a faithful smile.

Julian walked into the living room.

There she was.

Sat upon Oscar's lap. Him reading her a book about a tractor who was sad or something like that. His arm draped around her shoulders, her head nestled into his neck, the sun beaming through the windows as if it was shining specifically on them, like a large cylinder, bathing them in clear light.

"Oh, hey, man," Oscar greeted as he noticed Julian in the doorway. "There's coffee if you want some."

Hayley turned around and smiled.

"Hi, Julian," she said.

Julian didn't say a word.

"What's the matter, mate? You look awful. Not sleep well?"

Hayley smiled. Grinned, but with a childish nature, no malice. At least, not to the unknowledgeable eye.

"Yeah, I'm fine," Julian unsurely sputtered out.

He left the room, making his way to the kitchen, finding himself dizzy, falling against the walls. He stumbled to the sink, filled a glass of water, put it to his lips, threw the contents down his unharmed throat, plunged it down his unscathed neck, not a single pinch of pain.

But then again, it wasn't his throat that should hurt, was it?

The television was on in the kitchen. A small television, with the volume low. He hadn't put it on, hadn't noticed it, but it was there, the news announcing itself.

"Father Johnny Cartwright was rushed to hospital this morning when discovered in his church," came the news reporter's voice.

Every hair on Julian's body stood on end. His head slowly turned. There, on the screen, was the face of Father Jensen, with his fake name beneath.

"Father Johnny Cartwright was well-known for being instrumental in his work with underprivileged children and had been awarded an OBE for his services by the queen."

Julian felt a sudden pang of guilt for knowing so little about the man he'd enlisted the help of.

"Doctors confirmed that he had died of natural causes, believed to have been a heart attack."

Julian smacked the off button with the palm of his hand.

A mouthful of sick lurched to his mouth. He spat it in the sink. Had more water.

He dropped the glass into the bowl.

Walked back into the living room.

Watched her.

He knew why that news report had been left on.

He didn't know how the timing had worked, how it had

161

been playing the exact moment he walked in, how she knew he would hear it, but he knew it was her.

Oscar kissed her on the forehead.

She turned and looked at Julian.

There was that smile again. Innocent and unmistakable.

Julian understood, then and there, that they were in a war.

And that they were losing.

THEN

## 3 2

THE ROUGH CONTOURS OF MARTIN'S HANDS TRICKLED OVER HIS face, wiping the sweat away, wiping the dismay, the hatred, the anger, wiping it all away.

Then his hands fell to his knees and it all swept back over him again.

Hospital gowns weren't flattering. In fact, at the exact moment you feel the worst, they are the one thing you'd least like to be wearing. Waking up, feeling like hell itself had scraped a thousand knives through the inside of your skull, like your body isn't yours and it's some tight entrapment of your soul, like your decisions have led you to one powerfully impotent moment – then you look down, see this fluorescent, unflattering gown draped over your perspiring pores; it's not what one needs in that moment.

He rolled to his side, seeking water from the side of his bed.
None.

He'd woken up in some rough situations before, but with his brain bumping against the inside of his cranium, this was right up there with a night on the streets or next-day pains of fighting the heir of hell.

"Are you after some water?" came a familiar voice.

Martin looked up. He hadn't even noticed Father Jensen sitting in the corner.

He didn't know what to think. What to say. This man had saved his life. This man had both rescued him and condemned him. This man had done everything in his power to avoid Martin's cut, limp wrists from bleeding the last piece of life from him, had denied him his sweet release that would have ended the agony of life.

So, not knowing what to say, he just replied, "Yes."

Jensen stood, walked outside, then re-entered moments later with a paper cone of water. He helped Martin sit up, lifting the pillow to support his back, then placed the cup of water in his trembling hands.

Martin placed the water to his lips and enjoyed every moment of its rich thickness cascading down his throat of knives.

Jensen pulled the chair closer and sat beside him. Watching him. Studying him.

Comfortable awkwardness sat in the air between them. A relaxed anxiety simmered.

"How are you feeling?" Jensen asked, finally breaking the silence.

Martin raised his eyebrows.

"Okay, bad question, I just wanted to say something. I can't stand silence."

"Yeah…" Martin answered, his voice unused, drifting into a croak.

"So, the doctors have said–"

"Why did you do it?" Martin interrupted.

Jensen responded with emptiness, then resolved himself to speak.

"Because you were going to die."

Martin scoffed.

"You know," Jensen persisted, "I could ask you the same question. Why did *you* do it?"

Martin looked at Jensen. Said nothing. Drank the rest of his water.

"You shouldn't..." Martin tried, his voice petering out. "You... you shouldn't have done it."

"Shouldn't have what?"

"Saved me. Stopped me. You should have just let me die."

"Well, I am afraid it is not within my job requirements to allow people to perish."

"Shut up. This had nothing to do with you being a priest."

"I'll have you know–"

"So why did you?" Martin lifted his eyes from his fidgeting hands to Jensen's brave face. Jensen's expression wasn't real. His body language was fake. Martin could see that. Jensen probably didn't even know why.

"Because I care about you, Martin."

"So you were being selfish?"

"And because you have a lot to offer the world."

Martin snorted and turned back to his hands.

"You do, Martin. You need to see that."

"No. I'm weak."

"You are not weak."

"I let that – that – baby, or whatever it was inside of Madeleina, I let it...take me. Wipe my mind of reason."

"Just as it would anyone else who was in your situation."

"Yes, but I am better than them – I *have* to be better than them. I'm part of heaven, aren't I?"

Martin's face had completely morphed. It was a look Jensen had never seen Martin wear. His face was painted with tears, adorned with worry, completely taken over by despair. This was finally a glimpse as to what was underneath, an insight into the real Martin; the scared little boy who got into fights at school and lost his mum.

Finally, the real Martin surfaced.

"At least you will know now, when other people are in a similar situation, what to do," Jensen said, and instantly realised what awful words of comfort they were.

"Fat load of good that would be."

"Why?"

"I'm done. How am I supposed to defeat hell when it infected me so easily?"

Jensen watched Martin. Watched as Martin wiped tears away. Watched as the weak teenage boy Martin had lost found him once again.

"You were too young when all of this started, I know that. Derek knew that. He did it because he had no choice."

"Don't talk to me about Derek."

"I am going to talk to you about Derek, Martin, and I'm sorry if you don't like it."

"Derek didn't help this one bit–"

"Derek is the strongest person I have ever met."

"Strong?"

"Yes, do you know why?"

"Why? Why would you ever describe that dickhead as strong? He screwed up."

Jensen leant toward Martin.

"Yes, he did. But do you know where he is now?"

"…Where?"

"Fighting demons. Because when he screwed up, as he has done many times before, he didn't cut his wrists. Because he couldn't. He had to be strong for everyone else. For Eddie. For you."

Martin sighed.

Jensen stood. Placed a hand on Martin's shoulder. Looked him in the eyes.

"A real man is not measured by his screw-ups, Martin. A real man is measured by how they do whatever it takes, whatever the costs, despite the many mistakes they've made."

Martin said nothing.

Jensen left, and they never saw each other again.

NOW

## 33

An unwashed shirt lay open on a bare chest. This wasn't an erotic exposure of a muscular torso – this was an unwarranted slip of bone, of marked skin poorly cared for.

A hand gently stroked the tip of a bottle, cursing it in the unconscious murmurs of sleep. Once the hand fell completely still, the bottle slipped, thudding against the tiles of the bathroom floor with a shuddering earthquake that broke him from his sleep.

His eyes opened.

Stinks of piss.

Where was he?

Toilet to his left.

Propped up against the wall.

Here, again.

He shook his head. The first time this happened he felt awful, pathetic, like a failure. Now it was an accustomed wake-up call. At least his face wasn't rested on the bowl. The last time he did that, he had to go to the corner store with a toilet seat imprint on his cheek that wouldn't come off no matter how many times he smacked and smacked and smacked his cheek.

He belched.

So what?

If a man burps in the bathroom and there's no one around to hear it, does it still make a sound?

His muscles ached with the strain of the excursion it took for him to drag his wretched body to his feet. His limp arms rested him precariously against the wall that felt unsteady, yet he knew it was solid brick.

He stepped forward, cursing as he kicked the bottle with his exposed toe. Fuck. That hurt. He meandered through to the empty fridge and noticed his trousers were hanging out the window.

Now. Did he do that to dry them because he washed them? Or did he do that to dry them because he pissed on them while he was wasted?

Honestly, it didn't matter.

She woke up in his bed. He watched her come around. It was nice of her to stay the night, though she really didn't need to. She didn't need to show that kind of customer service to make her stay.

Still, she was heavenly. Her bare black breasts rolled delicately to the side, her ribs rising and nestling, her curly hair spread out over the pillow in every direction it could.

"Oi!" he shouted.

She moaned.

God, even her morning groans were exciting.

"Wake up!"

Her eyes opened.

She looked at him. Startled. Like a morning bird about to sing.

"I paid you already," he stated.

"Oh yeah? How about some breakfast?"

He snorted.

Opened his arms wide as if to say, *Take a look around. Do I look like the kind of guy who has shit to make breakfast?*

"Oh," she acknowledged, leaning up and rubbing her eyes, unable to wipe the disappointment from her face.

Like he cared.

Who really cares about upsetting a whore?

"You can go now," he said, getting tired of waiting as he stared at her.

"Really?" she snapped.

"Yeah. Why wouldn't you?"

She held his eyes, as if she had an answer to that question. Honestly, he'd like to hear it.

"I heard you were great," she told him. "I heard you were a legend."

"Then you heard wrong, now sod off."

Shaking her head, she grabbed her dress from the previous night and stormed out in a huff.

Legend.

Was that what he was?

Legends are old. He felt old. But he wasn't.

Legends are tales you'd tell your grandchildren about.

Sure, he'd done great things you'd tell your grandchildren about. He'd defeated many demons and fought the heir of hell. But the problem is, children always want to know how the story ended.

Was this happily ever after?

At least Derek got that. At least Derek got to die a hero. At least he gave it his all.

Unfortunately for him, there was no more all left to give.

He turned on the television. Searched the cupboards for a packet of crisps or something, anything that would quell that acidic burning in the pit of his stomach.

Then the news came on.

"Father Johnny Cartwright was well-known for being

instrumental in his work with underprivileged children and had been awarded an OBE for his services by the queen. Doctors confirmed that he had died of natural causes, believed to have been a heart attack."

His head bowed.

Another person who died before he got to make amends.

Honestly, when was his turn?

Still, he should show his respect. Do something. Make the effort he didn't bother with when the guy was alive.

With a sigh, he put on his coat. Walked to the door.

Then it happened.

He caught sight of himself in his reflection. Hair askew, jacket ill-fitted, chin full of stubble.

He shook his head.

"You really are a dick, Martin," he told himself, then left.

## 34

Father Jensen's church was an hour-long trip out of Gloucestershire, but Julian felt it was his duty to take it.

That was probably the only thing he was certain of.

Too many other questions wrestled betwixt his inconclusive wonderings. Jensen had come to help Julian. If Julian had never found Jensen and implored him to give his help, Jensen's death would never have occurred.

Yet it was not with Julian's hands that Jensen's death had come to be.

So was it his fault?

His responsibility?

Was this man's death on his conscience?

Inside of Jensen's church, a tribute had been arranged. A picture of him smiling from his younger days sat in the middle of a board, surrounded by messages of love and praise and condolences that gave an unmistakable picture of what had been a great man.

Julian stood beside it for a while. Watching. Reading. Wishing he could have done something differently.

They were lost, he had no other way of looking at it.

As he turned to make his way out, to return to his car and drive back to his life of complexity, he passed a face that seemed vaguely familiar. A man in his late twenties, maybe early thirties; scruffy, a look of stubborn anger etched across his face.

Julian watched as this man walked toward the tribute and bowed his head, remaining there just as Julian had.

Then, as if bursting out of nothing, the sudden recollection made sense.

Julian had visited Derek's grave shortly after his death. As he stood there, he'd noticed someone behind him. He'd made eye contact. Then the man had walked away.

This was that man.

And, in that realisation, he understood who it could be.

"Martin?" Julian asked.

Martin looked to Julian, his expression not changing, then turned back to the tribute.

Julian walked to Martin's side.

"My name is Julian, I'm a friend of Derek's, I met Father Je–"

"I know who you are," Martin said, low and quiet, but strong enough to cut silence into Julian's words. "And I know why you're here."

"You do?"

"Father Jensen wrote to me. First time in years. He explained why you'd found him. Said I should do something."

"Then you have to help me."

Martin took a step toward Julian, inches from his face, and looked into him with the eyes of a man full of wrath, a man who had given up, a man who had nothing but resentment for Julian.

"Father Jensen died because he tried to help you," Martin spat. "Why would I do the same?"

Martin turned to leave.

"Because it's what Madeleina would want you to do," Julian declared.

Martin's feet ceased with a sudden sombre stance that told Julian he had either said something that was just right, or very, very wrong.

"What'd you say?"

"I have a friend who is just like you. He's in love with a woman, just like you were. And just like you both, they have a child, and—"

"I read his sodding letter, I know what the child is."

Martin turned. Looked Julian up and down. Whatever he was thinking, he was giving nothing away.

"Please," Julian pleaded. "We're at a loss. No idea what to do."

"How old's the child?"

"Over four months."

"Then you're fucked. The mother. How is she?"

"She's…bad. She's dying. She's not got long."

"Do you know why this is?"

"No. The doctors can't figure it out."

"Then you're thick as shit."

Martin walked over to a pew and sat down, removing his scarf and gloves. Although nothing was verbally said, Julian took this as his cue to join Martin, and did.

Their eyes both directed toward Jensen's tribute. Anywhere but each other.

"What's the lass's name, the mother?"

"April."

"The reason she is dying is because of the child. The child is a demon – not a child possessed, but a demon in human clothing. Something unnatural can't be on earth without a cost."

"You mean—"

"The child needs April to feed off, to stay alive. Once it has enough strength, it will replace April, take her place in this

179

world. And April will be sent to hell in its place. All just to balance the two worlds out."

Julian's gut twisted. So obvious. Yet so clearly not what he wanted to acknowledge. Did he really lack this foresight, or was this just pure denial?

"The child controls the father," Martin continued. "The father does its bidding. Somehow, the demon puts some kind of lock on his mind, makes him unable see the truth. Eventually, he will do anything to defend her. Including dying. Or killing."

"You mean, Oscar, he – he'd kill April?"

"If she became a clear risk to the demon's life, then, well, theoretically, yes. But she'll have been drained of life in a few months. It wouldn't make any difference. Then once the demon doesn't need the father anymore…"

"I – I don't know what to…is this what happened with you and–"

"You don't mention her fucking name, or what happened, that clear?"

Julian nodded.

"You want my help, you shut the fuck up, do what I say, and then wave me goodbye as I disappear and never have to speak to any of you fuckers again. Understood?"

Julian nodded once more.

"There's more. Your friend, the father, what'd you say his name was?"

"Oscar."

"Well, this link between the father and the demon… The mother is just the home for the baby, but for the father's part, he has helped create it. The demon has part of him with it. With Olivia, her baby was one month old, the control over the father was there, but hadn't had a chance to grow yet – which is why he managed to survive when the demon died. With your baby being four months, that connection is too engrained."

"So the demon will always control Oscar?"

"Not necessarily. Once the demon takes his proper form, its control over Oscar will be relinquished, it won't need him anymore. But their connection will remain. Their fate will be linked."

"Their fate?"

"As in, once the baby takes its demon form, yes it will relinquish its dominance over Oscar. But, with the demon being this close to its ascension, if it dies, so does he."

Julian watched Martin. He said these words so coldly, so matter-of-factly. It was as if Martin had spent a lot of time on working to keep emotions out of his life.

"So how do we stop it?"

"How do we stop it? You dumb as shit or what?"

"Well, I assume an exorcism wouldn't work."

"No, an exorcism gets rid of a demon from a human. This isn't a human with a demon inside, like I said, this is a demon. Nothing else."

Julian nodded.

Martin finally looked him in the eye. But it was a grave look, an emotionless glare. In a shuddering moment, Julian feared that this is how he would end up.

"So what do we do?" Julian asked.

"Ain't it obvious? There's only two ways to deal with it."

"What?"

"We kill Oscar after it takes full form."

"Or?"

"We kill it before it does."

## 35

THE HOUSE WAS COLDER.

It wasn't just the feeling of a chilly countertop. It wasn't just the occasional sight of April's breath hanging before her. Nor was it just the aching of her bones exacerbated by the icy air.

It was something else.

Something she couldn't describe.

A shift in the atmosphere. A tonal modification. A feeling that the rooms were emptier, the corridors longer, and the nights as drawn-out as the day.

She felt like a zombie, sat helplessly in a chair. Her illness had weakened her body, but her mind was aware enough to pay attention to the subtle changes. The way that Hayley clung to Oscar before he could deliver a kiss to April. The way that Hayley hogged his attention, the way he woke her up first, how he poured her drink with an enthusiasm she wouldn't let him pour hers with.

An outside observer would call it petty jealousy.

April knew better.

There was something else, some maleficent undercurrent, a wicked sense of evil and manipulation. More and more, as the days had gone by, Oscar looked like a puppet. Like the child was pulling his strings. Was controlling him through not only her words, her actions, her affections, but something else.

And there was the hatred. The understanding that Hayley was in charge and April was helpless, silently acknowledged between them.

Tea time. Oscar finished boiling soup. Poured it into a bowl. Gave Hayley hers. Poured it into a bowl for April, but Hayley spilt some, so April's bowl had to wait, Oscar had to clear the mess up.

And, as he did, Hayley kept her eyes in a dead focus with April. Held them with a callous smugness April couldn't define.

Oscar placed a bowl in front of her. Finally. After his faffing about.

She didn't touch it.

Her hands remained on her lap. Her eyes focussed on Hayley.

She didn't even care anymore.

This little wretch was systemically taking away her life, the relationship she'd worked hard for, the house she'd bought, the home she'd warmed. She couldn't fight her physically. And she hated it. She hated her. Hated everything about this situation.

Oscar scooped spoonful after spoonful of soup into his mouth.

April didn't flex a muscle or flicker an eyelash.

"Why are you staring at me, Mama?" Hayley eventually said, in that pretence of innocence she had concocted.

The lying little bitch.

"Mama, you're staring at me," she continued, playfully, as if it was a game.

Oscar looked up from his soup and noticed that April's eyes were transfixed, her expression deadly, full of rage, full of detest.

"April, you all right?" he asked.

"You," April muttered, her eyes not blinking, her face not faltering. "You…"

"What is it, Mama?"

"Don't call me Mama," she spoke in a slow, low voice, ridden with contempt.

"April!" Oscar scolded her.

"You nasty, disgusting piece of work."

"April, what's the matter with you?"

"You think you've won? You think I don't know? That the world won't know?"

"April!"

Tears glistened on Hayley's cheek.

"What's the matter, Mama? What is it?"

"Stop it," April demanded, her face fixed and her head shaking. "Just – stop it."

"Why are you saying this, Mama?"

"*Stop it!* I am *not* your mama! You are *not* my daughter!"

"April, what the hell is wrong with you?"

She ignored him.

"I will *kill* you. I will rip your scrawny, *little* throat out!"

"April, for God's sake!"

She ignored him still.

"You do not belong here."

Hayley's face dropped. The image of childish tears ceased.

"Fine," Hayley stated, definitely, precisely. "You want to do this?"

Hayley turned and looked at Oscar.

Oscar stood up, his joints moving mechanically, his face a blank canvas.

He marched to the kitchen drawer. Opened it. Shovelled his hands around the cutlery. Around the weapons.

Withdrew a knife.

"What are you doing to him?" April asked, her turn for tears.

Oscar lifted the knife into the air, looked to April, then thrust the knife into the kitchen cupboard with such force it went straight through.

He stood stationary. His hand still holding the handle. The blade still lodged in the wood.

"Are you my mama?" Hayley asked.

April shook her head defiantly. Tears like bullets, but she fought them, lifted her shield, scrunched her face into angry resolve.

"Are you my mama?" Hayley repeated.

April screamed at her. Opened her mouth and let out all that desperation, that wrath, that complete lack of ability or control over anything that was happening in her rapidly shortening existence.

Oscar ripped the knife out of the wall and held it out toward April.

"I won't ask again," Hayley stated.

"Fine," April said, barely audibly.

"Say it."

She heaved a breath out of her mouth, growling her frustration.

"I am your mama."

The knife dropped from Oscar's hand.

He sat down at the table and continued to consume his soup. Oblivious. Nonchalant. Just as he had moments before.

"And don't you forget it," Hayley whispered.

"This soup," Oscar declared, his joyous, enthused demeanour returned, "is bloody delicious."

April didn't have any.

Didn't touch it.

Didn't look anywhere but at the one she loved.

Stared at him, longing for him to meet her gaze, touch her, hug her, tell her it's all right. To put his arms around her and reassure her that he wasn't going anywhere, that he still loved her, that she was still safe.

He didn't look in her direction once.

JULIAN FLICKED ON THE KETTLE AND LEANT AGAINST THE kitchen side, watching April.

"You look tired," Julian observed.

"I haven't been getting much sleep," April said.

Julian poured the coffee, placed it in front of her, and peered through the hallway.

In the living room, through a few open doors, Hayley was on Oscar's lap, playing Lego. Attached to him as always. Together as always. Barely apart for a second.

Julian sighed. Oh, how he hated this.

Mostly, he hated what he was going to have to ask April to do.

He sat down and turned to her with his business face on. She knew this face all too well. She knew what it meant. And, in a way, she had been expecting it.

In fact, it was about time.

"Have I ever mentioned a man called Martin?" Julian asked. "He was a friend of Derek's."

"I've seen him mentioned in Derek's diaries. He was with Derek in the Edward King war, wasn't he?"

Julian nodded. Glanced back over his shoulder. Checked that Oscar and Hayley were engrossed in their singular existence. As always.

"I met him," Julian continued, lowering his voice to a quiet hush. "He met a child similar to this. He's fought this thing before. He's outside in the car. Waiting."

"Is he able to exorcise it?"

Julian solemnly shook his head.

"The demon's not in the child, April. It *is* the child. I'm sorry."

"But…" April's mind worked slower these days, but she realised what this meant almost instantly. "That means the only way is to…"

"To kill the child."

A moment of understanding passed between them. Old friends. Friends who knew each other so well, words were rarely needed to convey their thoughts.

"Oscar won't go for it," April pointed out.

"Oscar can't know. The demon has a hold on him, Martin said it did it before, that the demon controls the father, makes him into their, like, protector."

"So what do we do?"

He checked over his shoulder once more.

"We drown her. At the lake."

He let these words settle for a moment.

"The only way to do this," he continued, "is to do it without Oscar. And I know how much I'm asking, and what it is I'm asking for, and if you think you can't do this, then that's fine – me and Martin can–"

"No. I brought it into the world. It needs to be me. I need to be there."

"Okay." Julian nodded.

A sombre mood settled between them. Resolved to do what

was needed, but saddened that the task had to lie in front of them.

"I'm going to have to knock him out. Then we'll take her. Okay?"

April's face scrunched into an ugly face of tears. Except she could never be ugly. And Julian understood. And he felt for her, he really did.

She turned her face away. Raised her fatigued arm and covered it.

"Hey," Julian said, putting his arm around her. "Hey, come on."

"I…" April's words were lost in the despair. She shook her head, hating this, hating that demon, hating everything.

"Look, April, I know this is hard."

"Julian, he…" It was her turn to look over her shoulder. There he was. Oscar. Taking care of his daughter. He would have made such a good father. He was everything a father needed to be.

"April, I know you love him. I know. But think of it that, well, you're not betraying him – this is helping him. For his own good. To save him. To save both of you."

"Please, just… I don't know… Give me a chance."

"A chance for what?"

"A chance to try and reason with him."

"April, it won't-"

"I know. I know it won't work. But please, at least let me try. Go occupy that… thing. And let me try. If it doesn't work, then…come in here and…"

She couldn't say it.

"Okay, April. One chance. That what you need?"

She shrugged.

"I hate this," was all she could say.

"I know," was all he could answer.

"Hey, April wants to talk to you," Julian said.

"Oh, okay," Oscar answered, looked at Hayley in his arms.

"I'll keep her occupied. You go."

Oscar nodded and walked through to the kitchen. Whatever this was, it couldn't last long. Julian and Hayley obviously didn't get on, and he couldn't leave them alone.

He entered the kitchen. Stood beside April. Ran his hand down her hair.

"Hey," he said. "What's up?"

"We need to talk about Hayley," April said.

Oscar saw her eyes. Red. Damp. The left-over moisture of tears.

"What's happened? What's the matter?"

"Oscar, she can talk with perfect diction. She can walk and run without a stumble. She is smarter than your average fourteen-year-old."

"I know, amazing, isn't she?"

"Oscar, that isn't amazing. It's inhuman."

"I'm sure they said something similar when apes evolved to humans, thought that was strange–"

"Oscar, please, think about this with some objectivity. This doesn't feel right. Surely you can see that?"

Oscar threw his arms into the air. Paced like a stroppy teenager.

"Why can't you just be happy with her? She has done nothing but love you since the minute you got home!"

"Oscar, please, do you even remember my pregnancy? Remember what that was like? The things that happened?"

"It was complicated, yeah–"

"Oscar, I bit a cat. I puked up a cross. I have been comatose and left so weak I can't move without help. Can't you see this?"

Oscar shook his head. More and more vigorously. Waved his wagging finger.

"Why are you trying to take this away from us?"

"Oscar–"

"All I want is to be a happy family."

"And we can be, someday."

"Someday? But for now, what? You just want to give her away?"

April didn't respond.

Oscar took a leap to a giant assumption.

"Oh my God, you think she's possessed, don't you?"

"She's not possessed."

"Then what?"

"She's a demon. She can't be exorcised. She has to be…"

"Killed?"

Silence.

"That it?" Oscar persisted. "You want to kill a child? That who you are now?"

April turned to the living room. Looked worryingly to Julian.

He stood. Walked over. Behind Oscar's back, picked up a stray piece of wood from the fireplace.

"I mean, seriously, April," Oscar said. "Do you really think I'm that stupid?"

Just as Julian went to strike, Oscar reached his hand out and grabbed the wood mid-air.

Hayley was stood up across the room. Her eyes red. Her mouth moving in perfect synchronicity with Oscar's.

"You know, I really didn't want to kill you yet," declared the two simultaneous voices.

Oscar pulled the piece of wood out of Julian's grasp. Turned toward him. Thwacked it into Julian's shin.

Julian fell to the ground, grabbing his leg, writhing.

"You weren't supposed to die yet."

He lifted the piece of wood. Held it with authority. Looked the woman he loved in the eyes.

"But things can change."

## 38

SOMETHING WAS WRONG.

Of course it was, something always went wrong.

People die.

People live.

People fuck up, then die, then you never get to speak to them again.

He couldn't rely on anyone.

Ever.

Derek. Father Jensen.

Martin bowed his head.

For Christ's sake. Get a grip.

He opened the glove compartment. Took out a sedative in the form of a nice, pointy needle. It may seem peculiar to the partial observer, but Martin considered a sedative to be essential to an exorcist's arsenal. Sometimes, it can be your last defence. It can mean life or death.

He got out of the car.

Stopped.

Looked around.

Nice neighbourhood.

Maybe he was being a little presumptuous?

He didn't know Julian. Maybe Julian wasn't a fuck-up. Maybe, any minute now, Julian was going to saunter out of that front door with the child over his shoulder, ready to do what was needed.

After all, Derek had trusted him.

Then again, Derek had trusted Martin.

Where's Derek now?

Rotting with the worms. Worms, as Hamlet stated, are the real kings. They are the ones who get the final bite of our skin, the final say in our body's end.

*Fuck me, I'm quoting Hamlet now. This is the kind of shit Derek would come out with.*

Maybe he was Derek now?

As in, Julian was in obvious need of help. Did he need to be the mentor? He was likely to be vastly more experienced. *Julian didn't even know how to recognise when a demon baby was manipulating its human father.*

Martin laughed.

Take that sentence out of context, and it pretty much sums up the bizarre life he's led.

He edged toward the house. Looked through the living room window.

The demon was there. He saw it. He recognised it. It wore a different face, but its essence was the same.

He shifted to the left.

He could see Julian further in.

With a piece of wood.

No, hang on.

That piece of wood was hitting him.

"Oh, for fuck's sake," Martin muttered.

Is the whole fucking world incapable?

He charged forward, kicking the door open, marching through the hallway.

As he entered the kitchen, a man only a little less scruffy than he was stood over a woman with purple hair in the wheelchair.

Oscar and April, he presumed.

Martin didn't hesitate.

Before comprehension could control Oscar's senses, before he could make any coherent thought over who Martin was or why he was there, Martin stuck the needle into Oscar's throat.

"Grab the girl," Martin instructed Julian. "We need to take her to the lake."

He helped Oscar to the ground.

He gave April a brief glance. "Hi, I'm Martin, nice to meet you."

She nodded. Cautiously.

"You!" roared the booming voice from the disguise of the little girl.

Julian had his arms around her, but she wasn't half giving a hell of a fight. Her legs kicked, her arms flung themselves around, her mouth chomped and chomped at the exposed skin on Julian's arms.

"Yeah," Martin acknowledged, looking cockily to the…girl. Thing. Demon. Whatever she was. He didn't care, just so long as it died.

"Can't you sedate it?" Julian cried, wrestling around on the floor, trying his best to contain it.

"Nah," Martin said, shrugging effortlessly. Stupid question, really. "It's not a human. It's a demon. Can't really sedate a demon. You're just going to have to pin it against the backseat."

"You get the demon! I'll get April!"

*Screw that.*

"Nah, mate, you're all right. I'll get her, you can get this one. After all, I think she likes you."

Martin gave the demon a cheeky wink.

"Martin…" its voice hissed.

It stopped thrashing. Julian kept it restrained, did not let go, kept his muscles tensed, ready, as if it was going to try and surprise him.

"Yes, Martin…"

Martin ignored it.

"You come to send me back to hell?" it taunted.

Martin ignored it.

"If you succeed, I'll make sure to tell Madeleina you say hi."

## 39

HUMAN SKIN IS SO WEAK. PATHETIC. TERCILE.

*Wish it could be shredded. Wish I could shred it like snakeskin. Show them. Show them who I am. Show them my real face.*

Screams roared in different pitches, tones, voices, everything at once, everything at separate times, low enough to shackle the doors of the car and high enough to screech into their ears as they covered them for safety weak pathetic docile feeble humans weak humans pathetic humans.

"Eaargh!"

Writhing, punching, seizing, kicking out at their legs, punching out at their chests. Just wait. Just wait 'til this skin is shredded. Just wait til the red eyes come out to play.

May look like an infant. Yes, may. Like a child. Fragile. Defeatable.

*But it's starting to happen.*

Forcing it. Earlier than expected, yes. But needed. Essential. Not ideal. But to unleash the demon beneath, to unleash this true form, is to relinquish the humans of their control, of their strength over a feeble body, to release it.

April can die now. Don't need her.

Oscar will come. Once he wakes, he'll come. Protect her.

*I will kill him. Fuck her, then kill him. Pierce her insides with my claw. Run it through her chest 'til it splutters out her mouth with blood. Then pick her up on my claw and present her to Oscar as he sees what he let me do.*

"You can't... contain... me..." Each syllable came as a different scream, a different voice, each one menacing, intimidating, will not be intimidated, will not be menaced.

"I will fuck you..." It directed its child's eyes at April. Glowered red. "Oh, Mama, I will eat you from the inside..."

She looked so angry.

So upset.

Can feel it coming.

The change is coming.

Almost there.

"You're betraying him you know... You're... betraying him... and he won't forgive you..."

"Shut up!"

"April!" Julian shouted. "You must not talk to it! Don't listen to it!"

"Oh, mister big dick over there... you ever looked at it, Mama? You ever thought about it? Betrayed him with your mind..."

She turned her face away.

"I will...use his...on you..."

"Make it stop," she whimpered.

"April," came the wizened voice of Martin. "Come on."

Writhing, wriggling, the demon inside growing, ready to burst, it's almost here, ready, unleashing, almost. Taunt them. Keep them angry. Keep them reckless. It won't be long until they are inside out.

"Listen to him...April...he did have one of me before..."

A glance in the rear-view mirror. All Martin gave. All it needed to. Game face was on. But barriers were down.

"Derek…killed your baby…killed it before it could be me…"

Laughter. Booming laughter. Vicarious, screeching, piercing laughter, cracks in the windows, causing them, cracks in their resolve, weakening.

Growing stronger.

Can feel it.

Nearly there.

"Madeleina…" it stretched every syllable of her name out, like each one was a sharp nail across a chalk board. "Mad…e…lei…na…"

He looked forward.

Pretended.

Pretended it didn't hurt.

Fucking imbecile.

"I fucked her from the inside you know…"

*This'll get him.*

"Martin," came the voice, a pleasant voice, a woman's voice.

*Her* voice.

"Why did you let me die? Why did you let our baby die?"

"Shut up," Martin grunted.

Julian put his hand out.

"The baby fucked me from the inside," her voice continued. "And it tasted better than you, much better than you and your pathetic attempts to be a man…"

"Shu–" he stopped himself.

Stronger than thought, eh?

Stronger.

But weaker than he presented.

"Oh, you…" the demon's manic voices entwined into a chaotic orchestra, its disgusting voice resumed. "So fun…"

Martin's face. So stiff. So expressionless. So false.

"I tortured her… in hell… for fun…"

Nothing. Yet everything.

"Watched the devil himself fuck her, break her, rip her…"

"*Shut up!*"

"Yes, I got it! I got you… Got you…"

"No, you got nothing. And you're about to die. So *fuck* you."

"So easy…I got you, under my skin…"

Now it was singing.

"I got you, under your skin…"

A sudden bolt of a hand swept out and grabbed April, clutching the skin, sinking its infantile fingers into her breast, drawing blood, felt it, it was warm.

"I got you…under your skin…"

Julian turned around and punched its arm. Breaking the bone. Forcing it out of its childlike socket.

It peeled back.

Something came out.

Something inhuman.

Claws. Bigger.

It was happening.

"Martin…" he said.

"What?"

"Its arm…"

Martin looked in the rear-view mirror. It was changing. It's demon's arm was just the start.

They hadn't much time.

He sped up. Skidded around a corner. Ran a light.

Writhing enjoying hating loving feeling numbing everything all at once everything it's coming it's bursting out within the hour it will have happened within the hour it will have happened within the hour it will have happened and they all they all will every last one of them they won't see it coming they won't they won't.

It's time.

"By the end of the night," *I told them,* "you are all going to be dead."

The car halted.

Beside a lake.
The lake April recognised.
Their special place.
By the end of the night.
*That's my promise.*
By the end.

## 40

A SMIDGEN OF HARSH KITCHEN LIGHT.

The solidity of harsh kitchen tiles against the back of the skull.

A smidgen of haze, blurred with the memories that don't order into sense.

These are the ingredients it takes to wake a man from a sedative.

Oscar's mind reacted before his body. April's face projected like a cinema screen at the forefront of his mind. Her skin, eyes, lips, hair, the smell of her, the silk of her voice, the grace of her touch, her hands, her...

What had she done?

Oscar's hand twitched.

A bead of sweat jogged down his neck.

His eyes adjusted.

He sat up.

April. She was saying such crazy things, she was so irrational, she was...

"Oh, God."

*Hayley.*

He attempted to leap to his feet but only rolled like a pin. Using the nearest chair to steady himself, he pushed himself up, finding his legs, standing tall.

The living room.

He ran in. Looked around. At every bit of empty space. At every bit of vacant memory. Every bit of ever-present absence.

He ran up the stairs, taking them two at a time, dragging himself up by the bannister.

Her room.

Empty.

His.

The spare.

The bathroom.

Check them again. Check them all again. And downstairs. Check the cupboard, maybe she's playing hide and seek. But he knew the truth.

Julian. He'd attacked. Tried to hit him.

They had taken her.

*Why would they do that?*

She was a helpless, innocent girl, under his care, and her mother had betrayed her, betrayed him. Julian had been in on it.

*Julian.*

And Oscar thought they were finally becoming friends. Since day one Julian had had it in for him. Was this what it took? Coercing April into kidnapping their daughter?

Were they with each other?

All this time. Friends. A relationship like siblings.

Something hidden.

*How could they?*

And there was a third person. Someone who'd put the needle in his neck. Someone who'd said something just before everything faded.

*Grab the girl. We need to take her to the lake.*

Grab the girl.

Hayley.

Take her to the lake?

There was only one lake Oscar could think of. But surely April wouldn't taint it? She wouldn't ruin the place that was theirs, where they had fallen in love, where they had…

No.

It was the perfect place for her betrayal.

If she and Julian wanted to rub it in his face, why not take her to the place where he felt most emotionally susceptible?

"Oh, God."

Again, another realisation lurched up his throat, bypassed his mouth and launched a rocket into his mind, exploding into a million notions of impenetrable truth:

*They are going to drown her.*

He ran to the kitchen side. Grabbed the car keys out of the little pot, the little pot he'd bought with her, the first thing they'd gotten when they moved in, when they were excited, when they were *in love.*

He opened the kitchen drawer. Grabbed the knife.

He burst through the hallways.

Bashed from wall to wall.

Shoved on his shoes without tying the laces.

Ran out the front door without thinking about locking it.

Met the driver's seat of his car. Turned the ignition. Ignored the seatbelt.

Hit the accelerator.

Hit it hard. Full throttle.

Traffic laws didn't apply to him.

Not today.

Not now.

It wasn't far. He'd be there soon. He'd be on time.

*Please, be on time.*

They couldn't have done it yet.
Could they?
"Oh, God."
Hayley.
*I'm coming for you.*

## 41

April felt like her own shadow. Following her body around.

Everything sounded like it was underwater. Voices blurred into other blurs.

Julian tried to help her out the car, put his arm around her, pulled her out, but all she did was fall.

"April," Julian said, shaking her. "April, come on."

She lifted her hand up. At least, she thought she had. God knew if she had. But she was trying to.

"April, come on."

"Julian," Martin prompted with a sense of urgency. "Julian, if we don't do this now, she has no chance. This is the only way to save her."

"I can't just leave her!"

"You have to."

Julian turned back to her. Shook his head. Shook it more.

Suddenly, he was seeing her again, younger, so much younger. An innocent face on the streets. A teenager who hadn't had a house for months but, in truth, hadn't had a home in years. A girl who would rather face the street than face her troubles. A girl with no family.

Then she became his family.

He saw her learning. Harnessing her gift. Growing with it. Helping people. He saw her becoming a woman.

Then he saw her with Oscar.

And he finally saw her happy.

"Julian," she managed. "Please… Just go…"

"I'll come back, I promise. Once we've done it."

"Oscar will wake up soon," Martin pointed out.

Julian held her hand until he was out of reach.

Then they were just blurs. Colours melding into movement.

She rolled over, onto her side. Why not? She sniffed in a breath, then found it caught, refusing to come back out again. She forced it out, but it came with a croak.

She felt herself crying.

The only thing she saw was Oscar. And their future.

A proposal. He's taken her to a restaurant. Spanish. Tapas, her favourite. She doesn't like to make her private life public, so he's hired out the function room. After the meal, he takes her there. It's adorned with flowers. Lilies, roses, daffodils. So many colours, so many smells. He gets down on one knee.

Their wedding day. He wears a purple cravat to match her hair. He smiles at her and she's never seen him so handsome. She surprises him by getting the conventional wedding dress, and he tells her that he's never seen her so beautiful. Her father isn't around to give the speech, so Julian does it, talks about how he and Oscar never got on, but he sees how much he loves her.

They have a baby.

A real one.

She's gorgeous. They call her Lily Rose, like the flowers he proposed next to. She doesn't start talking until she's eighteen months old. Like a normal child.

And her death bed.

When they are both old and grey.

He holds her hand. Tells her of the amazing life they've had. Thanks her for the amazing places she's taken him.

She tells him that she didn't actually do anything.

He says, "Yes. You did."

He doesn't let her go until the end.

It all faded.

Oscar appeared above her. His face was unrecognisable. It was red with anguish, torn with hurt. He was betrayed, and she knew it. She wanted him to save her, but he didn't.

Because he hated her. She could see it.

He hated her with every fibre of his being for what she'd done.

"Where is she?" Oscar asked, standing over her, seeing that she was dying, but not caring. "Where is my daughter?"

"She's not your daughter," April uttered, though it took a lot of strength.

Oscar crouched down beside her, placed his hand over her throat, and squeezed.

"Where is our daughter?"

In his eyes, she saw nothing of him. The child was not possessed, but he was. She was pulling the strings entirely. He was gone.

He was no more.

"Where. Is. She?"

His hand got tighter.

She was already losing life. It made no difference.

"I love you," she managed.

A baby's cry echoed in the distance.

Oscar stood up. Turned in the direction of the lake. *Their* lake. The one that was just across the field from where they were.

He picked up April.
He ran.

JULIAN HELD THE DEMON WITH A FIRM SECURITY HE WOULD NOT relinquish. Strange, looking into its eyes even though they were red, and its face had lost all its innocence, all he could see was the same young child.

They stood atop the bridge. Above the lake's deepest point.

Julian looked to Martin.

"It's time," Martin stated.

He still couldn't do it.

It was still a child.

"Stop!"

Oscar approached from the end of the bridge.

Hayley smiled.

Julian rushed to the edge of the bridge and held the writhing body, a child with a demonic arm, a toddler with red eyes, and suspended it over the side.

"Don't come any closer!" Julian demanded.

"Julian, what are you doing?" Martin asked. "Just throw it in."

Oscar stopped walking. He had something in his hand. He was dragging something behind him.

It was April's ankle.

"Oscar…" Julian gasped.

Oscar crouched beside April and held her head up. Her eyelids drooped as she stared absently at Julian.

Oscar placed the kitchen knife next to her throat.

"You know I can't let you do that," Oscar said.

"Oscar, let her go."

Oscar slowly shook his head.

"Oscar, that is April. You love her."

"Let my daughter go."

"Oscar, come to your senses!" Julian whimpered. "It has red eyes, it has a demon's claw; how can you not see it? Are you really so under its spell?"

"Put the child back on the bridge."

Hayley laughed.

"What you going to do…" it taunted between its chuckles.

"I will count to five," Oscar stated. "Then I will slit her throat."

Julian couldn't believe it.

That it had come to this.

"One."

Oscar, the timid boy hooked on anxiety medication. Discovered. Trained. Given purpose. The social reject who'd found his dream girl.

"Two."

April's eyes closed.

She was fading away.

"Three."

His grip on the demon loosened. He began to lift her back over.

"Four."

"Okay, okay," Julian said, and placed the child back on solid ground.

Hayley and her father looked each other in the eyes.

Reunited.

Happy again.

He dropped the knife and opened his arms for a big hug.

Martin sighed.

"Fuck this," he said.

He grabbed Hayley and leapt into the water.

## 43

THIS WAS IT.

The final full stop.

The final curtain.

The final the end.

Martin resisted the temptation to swim, to race to the surface, to recover some breath. He just allowed himself to sink. Holding tight. Further. Deeper. Toward the bottom.

Toward salvation.

In his arms, Hayley thrashed.

No.

In his arms, *Lamia* thrashed.

The one exposed demon claw grabbed his head, twisted it, trying to rip it off, tried to tear it, make him stop.

The demon didn't realise.

There was no point in placing the threat of death upon Martin. This was his intention. This was what he had decided.

He had to see it through. See it to the end. See that it worked.

He kicked his feet, kicked them at the water, they were

above his head, facing oxygen, so he kicked to force himself further away.

It tried to scream. Tried to bellow its multiple voices but it got lost on a mouthful of water.

Martin choked. His body wanted oxygen. There was no way he was getting it.

*Is this what it feels like to die?*

Hayley thrashed, but he put whatever life was left in his body, whatever life was quickly seeping out of him, into holding the body tight.

The child's body. The demon's disguise.

People will hate him for this. When they recover his body, they will label him a murderer. The front pages will say he dove into a lake and drowned a toddler.

It doesn't matter.

Martin had never been one to care about the perception of others.

The world would see him however they wanted to see him. He knew the truth.

As would anyone else who mattered.

Looking down on him.

Watching him. Waiting for him.

This was it. He was coming closer.

The child stopped fighting. The demon inside giving up. Losing its ability.

Its body grew limp.

Martin let it go. Let it wander away from him. It was still now, there was no more threat.

He could still climb to the surface, give himself a racing chance, bring himself back.

But for what?

For them to put him in prison? Bloody his name?

His body convulsed.

He choked and choked and choked and choked, his body

trying to breathe in, trying to take in oxygen, but getting nothing but water. It was entering his lungs. He could feel it.

It hurt.

Fuck, it hurt.

But it was the large pain before the sweet release.

He couldn't see the surface anymore.

He smiled. His body shot in various directions, as he began to seize, his vision was hazy, fuzzy, going, nearly gone. But he smiled.

*Are you there, Derek?*

Heaven would look upon this act favourably. The world's media no longer concerned him.

His eyes closed.

He was about to pass out.

Pass out, then it was done.

The audience has given their applause and left. The singer has completed their encore. The author has written their final word.

There were no tears.

This was not death. This was redemption. Don't mistake it for anything else.

*Are you there, Madeleina?*

His body stopped struggling.

He thought no more.

THEN

## 44

MARTIN WAS ON HIS KNEES FOR THE FIRST TIME IN HIS LIFE.

Funny, he fought for heaven, but he'd never prayed to it.

He was God's representative, but he never considered Him to be a friend. He was a boss. The owner of the business. The man that gave him the job then sat in the office, alone, watching everyone carry out their jobs whilst He reaped the rewards.

Martin placed his hands together. Closed his eyes.

What was he supposed to pray for?

Death? Help? Guidance?

No, he knew what he should pray for.

Madeleina.

"Dear Lord, please hear my prayer," he started, hesitated, rued himself for doing this, then continued. "Please keep her safely in heaven. Please make her happy. Make her at home. Tell her I love her. Tell her…"

No.

A large sigh brushed out of his lips.

Is that what he wanted?

For Madeleina to be safe?

Yes, of course. But for him, that did nothing. That gave him nothing. Such prayers were for show, to make you look honourable; they weren't truthful, weren't real.

"Dear Lord, please hear my prayer," he tried again. "Madeleina has a beautiful spirit, please place her highly in heaven, let her know…"

No.

Martin screamed. Stood. Threw a Bible across the church.

A few people sat on pews further back looked at him. He looked at them and they averted their uncomfortable gaze.

He didn't want Madeleina in heaven. He wanted her by his side. To tell him she forgave him. To tell him she was fine. That it was all okay.

Was God even listening, anyway?

Upon that thought, a sudden change in weather filled the church. Grey clouds outside the window parted and a large, glowing sun punished the window with its rays. It shone on Martin and he felt warm, felt every bit of his skin alight with heat.

He fell to his knees.

Faced the sun.

Bowed his head and placed his hands together.

"Dear Lord," he began.

He sighed.

He had no idea what words were about to come out.

But he decided he just had to let them.

"Dear Lord," he tried once more, "please hear my prayer."

He shook his head. Quelled his tears. Closed his eyes.

"Please bring me to Madeleina," he spoke in his first honest prayer. "Never mind keeping her safe, or keeping me safe, please, just…keep us together. If this means ending my time on earth and bringing me to heaven, then so be it. Please, just don't let us be apart. Let us be reunited. Our hands joined. That way I can tell her myself that I love her. Ask her to forgive me.

All I want is to hold her once more. So, if you can hear me, then…"

He paused.

Opened his eyes. Looked up to the sun.

"Amen."

He stood.

The sun departed, grey clouds obscured the window, the church was cast in shadow once more.

He turned and walked. The patter of his gentle steps carrying him out, through the doors, and into the rain.

Someday, his prayer would be answered.

NOW

# 45

Within minutes, the bodies had floated to the surface.

First, the demon's disguise, the child's body, bobbing, halting. Floating, with just its face and its belly visible. Her eyes wide open.

Then came Martin's body. His eyes closed. His fingers still. Nothing left.

Julian stared at the bodies. He said nothing. Nor did anyone else.

Oscar watched as they resurfaced. A paradox of emotions filled his body and threatened to burst out. The veil was lifted and beneath it, there he was. Angry. Resentful. Regretful.

Everything he'd done.

He remembered it.

The knife. Against April's throat.

*Oh, God...*

April stood. Walked to the edge of the bridge. The only aching she felt was from being sat in one rigid position for so long. Her strength returned with full vigour, but her resolve remained weakened.

She wiped a tear away.

She cried, but for what? Martin's death? Hayley's demise? For being trapped in a wheelchair whilst she watched Oscar plunged into becoming a minion?

They didn't look at each other. Not at first. For longer than they could stand, they stood eerily still, staring anywhere but at the other person.

Eventually, April's face lifted, her eyes directed at Oscar.

He didn't return the gaze. How could he?

He bit his lip.

He couldn't cry. What would that show? Look at what he'd done. The mess he'd created. The treatment of her.

To cry would be to patronise the whole situation. To demean his actions, to pretend that he was the victim.

But that's how April saw him. She knew that she'd have ended up doing the same.

"Oscar," she spoke, ever so softly.

Oscar shook his head.

"Oscar, please, look at me."

He tried. He lifted his head, but a mind full of heavy thoughts weighed it down.

She turned toward him. Walking into his body space. Placed a hand on his face.

He removed it. Turned away.

"Oscar, it's over. Please, just–"

"It's over?" Oscar retorted. "How could this be over?"

"Oscar, please."

"How could we just go back to our lives after this? Don't tell me you want to pretend it's all okay. That we could just throw away our memories, just…"

His voice caught in his throat.

"I'm not saying anything," she said, her head lilting, pain watering her eyes, longing, wishing he would just look at her.

"You killed my daughter," Oscar stated.

"You know that's not true. You can see it now, can't you? Surely?"

"I...I don't know what I see."

"Oscar, please. I love you."

This time he did look her in the eyes. Lifted his head, held her gaze of agony, looked over her and did not know what to think.

"Oscar?" she asked, waiting to hear those words come back to her, waiting to feel his arms around her.

But her body remained cold and unembraced. Her heart remained beating fast, but for her, only her.

"Oscar, after all we've been through, do you not... Do you still love me?"

"I–"

He grew angry and tried to quell it. After everything, did she really think you could just end it like that? Sum it up with three small words, as if that undoes everything?

But, in truth, she did.

"Oscar..."

"April, stop."

"Oscar, we are Sensitives. This is the war we fight, and we need to be strong to fight it. We need to be above all this. We need to be able to fight hell, win, and still love each other."

"It's not that simple."

"It is, Oscar. It really is."

"April, think about this."

"Oscar, do you still – do you still love me?"

He thought. He knew the answer, but it would not meet his lips.

"I–"

"Guys!" A sudden interruption from Julian prompted them to leave their lamentation.

The water's surface bubbled and boiled like a cauldron. Simmered, like the whole lake was in a pan. Steam rose.

Then, from the depths of the water, something fired out and hovered in the air before them, masking the entire surroundings, hiding the peaceful night sky with its fiery hands.

From its waist downwards a large, thrashing tail, snakeskin decorating its length. Its thickness and its strength smashed the bridge's solid brick surface in a way that forced April, Oscar, and Julian to flee to the nearby field.

Its tail smacked the ground next to them and the vibrations thrust the three puny humans onto their backs.

Its eyes glowed red, its mouth open to reveal its fangs, sharp enough to pierce glass. An embellished diadem ornamented its head, impressive carvings forming its sinister shape. Its naked torso boasted two large breasts, protected by jewels moulded into decorative points, points harsh enough to draw blood.

Its arms lifted into the air, two pronounced sets of claws atop them, nails twisting into weapons, contorting into instruments of death.

Its smile curved into a grave omen.

Its tongue, hissing in a sick silence of satisfaction, flickered into two parts.

Oscar wanted to run.

April wanted to flee.

But Julian knew what they needed to do. He would not let the star-crossed lovers escape their final task.

The demon looked upon them, and they all knew instantly who it was.

This was what had been growing inside her. What had been twisting and writhing beneath the surface.

Hayley wasn't needed anymore.

It had promised that within the hour, it would arrive.

And it delivered.

Lamia had delivered.

## 46

JULIAN WAS NOT AFRAID.

He couldn't be.

These were the eyes he'd looked into for four months and thought – *I will not let you win.*

This was the time to prove that.

So he couldn't be afraid. He couldn't let himself. He would not.

Oscar and April cowered behind him.

Understandable, maybe. It had made April into a weak, empty shell of a person. It had made Oscar into a deluded puppet.

Julian remained the only impartial enemy.

He stood. Took the cross that hung on a pendant from around his neck and presented it to the beast.

It laughed. No, it guffawed.

"Julian…" Lamia hissed. "Oh, Julian…"

"The cross may be small, but the spirit is not."

The beast opened its salivating jaw and forced three booming snorts of laughter to echo from its fateful, bloody lips.

Its decedent belly convulsed with humour, pathetic mocking of the pathetic human with his pathetic weapon.

"I watched you…" Lamia growled. "For months… Waiting for this… Waiting to kill you…"

"Try it."

Julian held the cross tightly, just as he had done for hundreds of exorcisms. Yes, this demon wore a different mask, it wasn't inside a child, or an innocent conduit – but it was still the same enemy. Its appearance could not shake him. He couldn't let it.

"Almighty God," he began, "cover my mind with the helmet of Your salvation, reminding me constantly that I am Your child and the enemy can't mess with me."

Lamia left the lake, thrashing its tail and bringing it down with a shuddering impact, forcing Julian onto his feet, and for April and Oscar to momentarily rise into the air. They crawled back, backing away.

April took hold of Oscar's hand in hers.

He let her.

Julian stood tall. Stood firm.

"Get behind me," he told the other two.

Normally, with what he expected from them, he would have scolded them to no end with intense disappointment for backing out of a fight. But he knew what it was like to be held by a demon, to be trapped by it, to be completely taken to the point that he couldn't see the truth or any resemblance of it.

No. For now, he would be their protector. He would be their saviour. They could thank him later.

Julian paraded himself before the demon, holding out the cross, a few feet away, so close, all it would take would be one swipe, one plunge of the claw, and his demise would be met.

But he couldn't think of the imminent death.

He had to think of the prayers. The protection. It was the only way to fight it.

"Fix my thoughts, Lord, on what is true, honourable, right, pure, loving, and admirable," he persisted.

The demon thwacked the cross out of his hand, sending it disappearing into the night.

Julian held out his hands. Made a cross with his body. Stood firm.

"Your peace will guard my mind!" he said, screaming it, bellowing it, using his body as his tool, as his cross, hoping it would work, ignoring the doubts, ignoring that thought at the back of his head. "Then I will learn to recognise Your will for me, which is pleasing, which is perfect."

The demon roared with hysterics.

It slashed out its claw, marking it across Julian's chest.

He fell to his knees, his t-shirt ripped. He looked down. Blood dripped onto the grass. A large gash on his chest, stinging, burning like hot coals.

"Saturate my mind with Your truth," he continued, but the words were weak. The pain was harsh. He was going to pass out, he could feel it.

He lifted his hand from the wound, finding it drenched in dark red.

The blood was dripping down his waist.

"I am convinced," he tried, spluttering the words, wincing from the agony, "that the answers are found in Your world, not out in the world."

He fell to his knees.

April went to help him, but Oscar put his arm across her.

"Lord, keep the enemy at bay–"

Lamia's giant claw swiped and knocked Julian through the air, like a tennis ball thrown from father to child. He landed on his back and groaned.

He couldn't go on.

April went to stand, but once more, Oscar stopped her.

"What are you doing? It's going to win."

"You can't defeat it, April."

"Are you still disillusioned? After this?"

"No, you don't understand."

Oscar stood tall. Staring at the beast. Staring at the thing he'd been protecting for so long.

He hated himself more than he ever had.

"Only I can kill it," Oscar stated.

"What?" April gasped, refusing to let him walk into death so easily.

"It's me the demon's had the link with. It's only me that can do anything."

Lamia's mouth curved into a smirk.

"Get Julian to the hospital."

"Oscar, I'm not leaving–"

He took hold of her hand.

"Just do it. Trust me."

April paused. Looked into his eyes. Looked at the sincerity that had returned. This was the first time she'd seen those eyes in so long.

She ran toward Julian, helped him to his feet, helping him to limp away.

"Okay," Oscar said, walking steadily toward Lamia.

"Hello, Dada," it said, cackling as it did, tormenting, just continuously tormenting.

Oscar shook his head.

"No," he said. "Not anymore."

THE MOMENT APRIL ANNOUNCED SHE WAS PREGNANT.

The concerns he'd had about her welfare.

Derek dying as he stopped her from killing herself and the child.

The day she gave birth.

Taking Hayley home without her.

Learning to be a parent without her.

How hard it was, missing her, trying to be a dad, but needing her, needing help, struggling, struggling so much.

Loving that child.

First walk.

First word.

April waking up.

Being a puppet for a demon parading around as a child.

Everything. Every thought, every second, every piece of hurt. Every awful thing it did. Everything awful thing it made him do. Every moment he was oblivious to the pain he was causing to the woman he loved.

Every single thought and feeling channelled itself into his

words, and the venom was articulate and pronounced in a way that the demon could not perceive.

"Lord God, captain of my heart, Satan knows if I follow your greatest commandment."

Lamia looked perturbed.

It didn't understand.

But Oscar was starting to. He was realising how he could win.

How he was going to win.

And it made him smile.

"It is powerless over me. Guard my heart, it beats for her alone. You empower it."

Oscar stepped toward Lamia.

The large, towering, infernal beast backed away. The visage of mockery and deceit, cowering for a reason it was yet to comprehend.

"Remove the idols from my mind so that You alone can command my allegiance. Give me not a foothold in my enemy or hate or bitterness on my part."

He spread his arms out. As a cross. As a man baring his soul. As the world's greatest defence.

"Cultivate my heart in You that bears all things, believes all things, hopes all things, and let this unclean demon know it will not win."

"Stop!"

"Let it know it's power over me is diminished. I am hidden with You, hidden away from it, and it will not win."

"You…"

"You will *not* win!"

The demon's claw sliced through the air, aiming for Oscar's throat, soaring through like a razor blade in a fiery trail.

Then it halted. Inches from Oscar's neck.

Hovering.

About to strike, but not.

"Do it," Oscar instructed.

The demon looked back at him. Unable to understand why it resisted.

"Go on."

"What – what are you…"

"You planted yourself in me as my puppet master. You have been in control of me from the inside. You can't do that without any side effect."

"What…side effect? How dare you–"

"So if you slice my throat open right now, the throat you have been holding with your strings, what do you think will happen to *you*?"

"You…you lie!"

Oscar took a step forward.

The claw pressed gently against his throat. One slight push and blood would seep out and he wouldn't be able to breathe and it would all be over.

"Why don't you try it?" he asked, a cocky sneer lifting his grin. "Why don't you find out?"

Lamia's face tightened, a contortion of anger.

Oscar grabbed hold of the claw. Held it tightly. Pulled it closer against his throat. Began to feel its sharp sting against his oesophagus. Feeling its imminent flourish against his gullet.

"Kill me," Oscar said. "Or go back to hell where you belong."

Lamia readied itself for the strike, to plunge its claw further in, to kill him.

But it didn't.

It couldn't.

Like an obedient daughter, it did what it was told.

"This isn't over," it told him.

"Yes," Oscar replied. "It is."

It withdrew its claws and in a sudden cry of anguish, it roared its anger to the sky. Morphing into a ball of flames, it plunged downwards, hitting the earth, going deeper, deeper, deeper.

Oscar stood alone.

It started to rain.

He looked around himself for April. But, like he'd demanded, she'd gone.

It was over.

He shook his head.

How could it be?

Just look at what he'd done.

The demon was gone, but it wasn't over.

And it never could be.

TWO WEEKS LATER

OSCAR OPENED THE FAMILIAR DOOR WITH A TOUCH THAT NOW seemed alien.

The creak felt no longer his, the mat he wiped his shoes on not home to his dirt, and the warmth of the hallway only chilled him.

He dumped his bag on the ground.

Walked through to the living room.

"Hey," he said.

April turned and looked at him.

She looked different. She was the same, but her strength had wiped itself away. He could tell she had spent most of the last two weeks crying, he knew her that well – but he also knew her well enough that, being the strong woman she was, she wouldn't wish to acknowledge it.

"I made you a cup of tea," she told him.

And she had.

His favourite cup sat on a small coffee table to the side of his side of the sofa. He placed himself down on it beside her. It felt firm, unused.

"Thank you," he said, not knowing how to begin this

conversation. He took a sip to further delay words. It was still hot.

As he looked toward her, he noticed that her favourite cup was empty.

"How have you been?" Oscar said, then immediately felt stupid for it. "I mean, I know it's only been…but…I don't know. I don't know what to say."

Her eyes remained on him. That look she reserved only for him, fixed to his face, only now it was different. Smudged.

"I've missed you," is all she needed to say, and all he needed to hear.

"I've missed you, too," he said.

He placed his hand on hers, which rested between them, the only thing crossing her boundary and his. Her thumb gently rubbed his finger. He returned the gesture, then withdrew his hand, keeping it on his side of the sofa.

"Are you feeling better?" he asked.

"Yeah, much," she answered. "My body ached from being so still for so long, but everything else came right back. I've never enjoyed the use of my legs so much."

Oscar smiled, then stopped. At first, he was endeared to her humour, then the seriousness of the situation hit him.

"I'm sorry," he said.

"You don't need to be."

"Yeah, but you were–"

"I was."

"And I–"

"I know."

"Don't I need to be apologetic?"

"I don't know what you need to be, Oscar."

"Then why am I even here?"

He stopped himself, quick, before he could feel the undue heat rising to his voice. The last thing needed was an argument. That wasn't how he wanted this to go.

"I want you to move back in," she said, cutting through the mist. "It's empty without you. I need you."

He nodded to the floor.

"Don't you think you need to apologise, too?"

"What for?"

"Sedating me? Going against me?"

"I thought you understood?"

"Yes, but you still…"

He closed his eyes and shook his head. He wished he could find the words. He knew anything he said was not going to be right, but he found the wrong words spewing out of his mouth nonetheless.

"I what?" April asked, keeping herself calm; there was no anger, only despondency. "What did I do?"

"It's not a simple situation."

"What?"

"I know what you did was right. I know it saved us. But it also broke a trust between us I never thought we'd break. What I did wasn't me, but when you betrayed me, when you went behind my back – that was still you, and I just…I can't get past that."

"But I did that to save us!"

"Try to understand."

"How are you even asking me this?"

"I knew I shouldn't have come back."

"Fine, Oscar, I'm sorry! Is that what you want? However it is you're feeling, betrayed, whatever – I'm sorry for it. Now will you move back in? Please?"

He couldn't look at her.

"We had a daughter," Oscar said.

"What?"

"For a brief time, we had a daughter together. And I didn't even think it could go so wrong."

"We didn't have a daughter, Oscar. It just looked like one. It was a demon. The whole time, it was a demon."

"I know that, but it was still – still ours. Ours to take care of."

"Oscar, please."

She pushed forward, broke the boundary, grabbed hold of his nearest hand in both of hers. Squeezed it. Reached out to him with her eyes, ran his fingers through her palms, leant toward him.

"Just come home," she insisted. "I love you so much."

"I love you, too."

"Then–"

"I love you, but…"

"But? But what?" She put her hands on his cheeks and turned his head toward hers. His eyes still met the floor. "There is no but."

"I'm leaving, April."

"Leaving? When?"

"Now."

She stared at him. She couldn't understand. How was he leaving? He had just gotten there.

How was this happening?

How was this even happening?

"Oscar, whatever it is, we'll see to it. We'll sort it."

"April, you don't understand."

"Then make me."

"April, I was under the control of that thing for almost half a year. It made me obsess over it. All I thought about was it; I was ready to kill for it. I threatened you. I put a knife to your throat, for *it*, for a *demon*. Don't you see how wrong that is?"

"Oscar–"

"And I can't go on without knowing why, why that happened, and why I wasn't strong enough to overcome it, why I couldn't recognise it, why being what I am still meant I couldn't see what I was doing to someone I love so much."

He took hold of her arms and placed them back on her lap.

"Oscar?"

"So I'm leaving. To find out."

"To find out what?"

"What this label even means. I want to know why I'm a Sensitive. What being a Sensitive is. And why it means nothing when controlled by – by a child-eating demon from hell."

He stood.

She stood too.

He turned.

She grabbed hold of his arm.

"Oscar, stay, we'll figure it out. We'll figure it out together."

He turned to face her. Finally. Placed a gentle kiss on her lips. Squeezed her hand.

"I'll let you know where I am, when I can."

He turned.

She ran after him.

He ignored her. Took his bag, walked through the door, and into the car.

It was all he could do to avoid watching her face disappear in the rear-view mirror.

## 49

THE TRAIN STATION WAS FULL OF HUGS. SOLEMN DEPARTURES. Happy goodbyes.

Oscar imagined he was going to war. These were soldiers kissing their wives and mothers goodbye. All on the same route. All to the same place.

But they weren't.

They were just ordinary people living their ordinary lives.

He took his seat, took out his headphones.

His mobile had a text message from April that he ignored. He knew what it would say. He didn't need to read it. Not now.

It wouldn't help him be strong.

And boy, did he need to be strong.

The train took off. Non-stop to London Stanstead. People waved goodbye out the window.

There were so many goodbyes, but Oscar supposed that's because of where they were heading. This wasn't your average train to work. This was your train to the airport. You wouldn't leave the country without a goodbye.

At least, most people wouldn't.

He selected his favourite playlist. *Epic Soundtracks.* Soon, the song from the end credits would be filling his ears, and he'd try not to get emotional. Following this would be his favourite tracks from his childhood movies. *Back to the Future. Star Wars. Indiana Jones.*

Those movies all made it look so simple.

The platform vanished and they entered a tunnel. The carriage was lit only by a dozen screens of a dozen mobile phones. Then they left the tunnel and it was bright and sunny again. No harm done by the darkness.

Oscar had never minded the darkness anyway.

The things that go bump in the night are a lot less scary once you've sent them back to hell.

He closed his eyes. Leant his head back. Tried to decide if he was doing the right thing.

He hadn't said goodbye to his parents. To Julian. To anyone but the person that mattered.

He pictured her now. Not crying, like he knew she was. But standing strong, like she always did in his thoughts. So powerful. Purple hair billowing behind her into the wind, hands on her hips, the superhero, the fighter, the powerful preacher no one would ever mess with.

A sudden pang of loss hit him in the chest.

And he saw himself with the knife in his hand, holding it against her throat, once again, like he'd seen so many times. It was like his memory was a polished desk with one carving in it, but it was a carving so deep and so engrained that there was no way to be rid of it.

What if he'd done it?

What if he'd–

He opened his eyes.

Maybe he wouldn't try to sleep.

Maybe he'd read a book. He'd always wanted to read a book, but he'd never had time. Now would be a good time to start.

Maybe some kind of guide to other countries.

Were they going to speak English?

He laughed. That's what he was worried about.

There were graver paths before him.

He tucked his phone in his pocket. Looked around at the people in other seats. Most of them travelling alone.

Then he turned to the window. Stared at his reflection. Met himself in the eye.

And that's where his eyes stayed.

He had questions. Lots of them.

He was a Sensitive.

As was April.

As was Julian.

And even if he had to ask the devil himself, he was going to find out what that meant.

# JOIN RICK READER'S GROUP AND GET THE DEMONOLOGIST HANDBOOK FOR FREE!

Join at **www.rickwoodwriter.com/sign-up**

THE SENSITIVES BOOK FIVE:
QUESTIONS FOR THE DEVIL IS
OUT NOW

# RICK WOOD

# WOOD

QUESTIONS FOR THE DEVIL

THE
SENSITIVES
BOOK
FIVE

CPSIA information can be obtained
at www.ICGtesting.com
Printed in the USA
LVHW110730261020
669800LV00006B/135